CLAIMING HER HEART

Under His Command Trilogy

Part Three

By Lili Valente

D1518288

CLAIMING HER HEART

Under His Command Trilogy: Part Three

Lili Valente

Table of Contents

About the Book

CLAIMING HER HEART
Under His Command Book Three

*Warning: Dominant alpha hero Blake
Roberts will own your nights and forever ruin
you for lesser men*

Blake has what he thought he wanted—Erin's
submission, her trust, and the woman he loves
back in his bed. But with her submission
comes protection of her secrets. Erin is in
trouble and an innocent life hangs in the
balance. Blake knows he can help her break
free of the past, but he doesn't know if a man
like himself belongs in her future.

How can he swear to protect her from danger
when he has a dark side of his own?

Author's Note

Blake and Erin's story is a fictional representation of a Dominant and submissive, BDSM relationship, based on research conducted by the author. In a real Dominant and submissive relationship, all sexual activity should be safe, sane, and consensual.

Dedicated to Lauren Blakely, Monica Murphy/Karen Erickson, and Sawyer Bennett. Honored to have the readership of such amazing, talented women!

ALSO BY LILI VALENTE

CONTROLLING HER PLEASURE

COMMANDING HER TRUST

CLAIMING HER HEART

Learn more at www.lilivalente.com

CHAPTER ONE

Blake

Erin was nearly naked again, wearing nothing but tiny black panties.

Her jeans had been soaked through or he wouldn't have taken them off. Blake needed her shirt off to get to the tattoo, but not her pants.

It certainly would be easier to concentrate if she were wearing more clothes and didn't

1

look so damned sexy spread out, face down, on the bed in his room. He still wanted her as much as he always had—probably always would—but the time for making love or fucking or whatever they'd been doing was over.

From this point on, he was all business.

Too bad this business had a lot in common with one of his favorite pleasures…

Bondage had always been a huge turn-on, even before he discovered the BDSM lifestyle. Either binding his lover or being bound himself, it didn't much matter. Both made Blake hard enough to shatter rock.

It was no surprise that his cock swelled uncomfortably within the confines of his jeans as he cuffed Erin's wrists to the mission-style headboard of the bed. He couldn't help being aroused, but he should have kept his hands to himself.

But he couldn't seem to resist tracing the column of her spine with his fingertips, past the small of her back and down both of her legs. He couldn't keep from gripping her just above the knees, digging his fingers into the soft flesh with the perfect amount of pressure, the kind he knew made Erin's pussy gush.

And then he pulled her thighs apart.

Wide.

Wider...spreading her open for him before he moved his fingers to her ankles.

A soft moan of excitement escaped Erin's lips as he knelt between her legs, making Blake's breath rush out softly in relief. Ever since he'd thrown her over his shoulder at the diner, he'd felt like a monster, a feeling that had only gotten worse as she continued to fight him all the way up to the cabin. With every passing second, he'd become increasingly convinced that he'd gone too far, crossed the line between consensual power exchange and being a goddamned bully.

But that sigh of arousal helped calm his fears.

No matter what she'd said in the diner or on the road up to the cabin, Erin hadn't been

3

faking her physical responses to his touch.

Her emotional response, however, was clearly another story. A story that made him so full of hurt and rage he saw red every time he thought about how easily he'd been played.

"See there, Erin. Aren't you glad I caught you in time?" His voice was as rough as the rope he used to secure first one ankle and then the other to the baseboard near her feet.

He'd only brought the one pair of cuffs so rope would have to do. At this point, the idea of rope burns on Erin's delicate skin didn't bother him as much as it would have two hours ago. It was amazing how badly it hurt to realize she'd been lying to him from the moment they'd arrived at the cabin.

He'd been a fool to believe the woman he'd *kidnapped* could have real feelings for him again in less than a day. No matter how much he cared for her, no matter how right it had felt to pick up where they'd left off eight years ago, it had been pure stupidity to drop his guard. He should have stuck to his original

4

plan from the beginning and spared himself the heartache.

And avoided abducting Erin from a public place. Again. You've really lost it, asshole, and chances are good you'll be facing criminal charges.

His inner voice was channeling Rafe this evening.

It was a pain in his ass and, unfortunately, probably right on the money. Even if the people in the diner didn't call the police to report what they'd seen, Erin now had several witnesses to corroborate her claims of being kidnapped.

A day ago, he would have said that it didn't matter, that he wouldn't have denied the charges anyway. After all the lies and deception he'd had to deal with growing up, he was more than a fan of the truth—he was a devotee. But now a part of him would be tempted to insist this weekend trip had been a consensual affair. He was *that* angry about being taken for a ride.

Or that devastated; take your pick.

He preferred angry. It hurt a hell of a lot less.

"Tell me, Erin," he whispered, his voice thick with anger. "Now."

He finished up at her ankles and moved over her prone form, bracing his hands on either side of her shoulders, hovering close enough that he could feel the heat of her body but not the silky softness of her skin. He moved his mouth just the barest bit closer, letting his lips brush softly against the back of her neck as he spoke again. "Tell me what you want."

Erin shivered, but he could tell it wasn't from the cold. She was aroused, he would bet his hands on it. If he let his fingers slide into those tiny black panties, he'd find her wet and ready, no matter how much of a fight she'd put up as he carried her up the stairs and wrestled her onto her stomach on the bed.

"Fuck you," she whispered, anger clear in her tone.

So she was pissed as well as turned on.

Good. That made two of them.

"I don't think so. No more distractions. We're going to finish this," he said, reaching over to where the tattoo machine sat beside the bed.

Blake flipped the switch on the motor then pulled on his latex gloves. He'd already prepped the gun with black ink and Erin's shoulder with an alcohol swab, so they were ready to go. All he had to do was put the needle to her skin.

He'd planned how he would modify the tat if Erin refused to give him her input, so there was no reason to stall. In half an hour, he could be finished and they could both be getting ready to head back to L.A. He should get on with it.

But for some reason, he couldn't force his hand to move any closer.

"Tell me what you want, Erin. This is your last chance," he said, hoping she heard the resolve in his voice. If she didn't talk now, she would lose the opportunity.

But she didn't say a word, only pressed her face into the quilt beneath her, every muscle tensed, bracing for the feel of the needle piercing her skin. The position only emphasized how small she was. Her wrists were tinier than ever, and her shoulder blades and the knobs of her spine were clearly visible through her skin, once more inspiring the desire to get to work fattening her up.

Fuck.

He should forget this insanity and go down and reheat the pasta, bring it upstairs, and they could eat it together in bed. They could feed each other tortellini and sips of red wine, then have each other for dessert. After all, who needed cheesecake when you could have your tongue buried in something as sweet as Erin's pussy?

The imagined scene made his cock twitch even as his throat grew uncomfortably tight. Nothing like that was ever going to happen again.

It had all been a lie, every touch, every

word.

Blake's anger sharpened to a knifepoint. Erin had let him think they had a future together and made him happier than he'd been in years, only to tear him down hours later. She'd *cried* in his arms, for God's sake, wept because she was so overwhelmed by what she was feeling.

Except now he knew she hadn't been feeling anything at all. It had been an act to trick the asshole still stupid enough to be in love with a woman who couldn't give less of a shit about him.

A second later, Blake dropped the tattoo gun to her pale flesh, tracing the edge of the wing he intended to expand. He'd add enough feathers to cover the angel's body, then go to work on the face, covering the ethereal features with wild strands of black hair. By the time he was finished, no one would recognize his tat and Erin's as similar, let alone matching in every detail.

And when the resemblance was gone, he'd

finally be free of this obsession that had haunted him his entire adult life.

"Stop," she sobbed.

"Sorry, I can't." He clenched his jaw, refusing to acknowledge the guilt that whispered through his rage. Screw guilt. It wasn't going to get this job done.

"Stop it. Stop!" The words started as a whisper but ended in a scream. Erin's shout echoed off the walls of the bedroom, followed closely by the horrific sound of a woman crying.

No, she wasn't simply crying. She was wailing like her heart was breaking, weeping so hard her shoulders shook as the sobs wracked her body, ensuring there was no way he could continue the tattoo. She was shaking too badly, but more importantly, she was obviously in serious emotional distress.

He might be angry with her, but he wasn't a monster.

You're not? So, you'll strap a woman down, but not sit on her to force her to hold still.

What a fucking gentleman.

Shame swept through Blake's body like a blast of cold air, shocking him to the core.

Jesus. What was he doing?

How could he have thought he'd really be able to go through with this against Erin's will? It was madness. What's more, it was cruel. No matter what Erin had done, no matter how she'd made him feel, he was supposed to be better than this. At least, that's what he'd always told himself.

Now…he wasn't so sure.

Right now, he was behaving more like every piece of shit foster father he'd ever had than he'd imagined possible. If he looked in the mirror right now, he knew he'd see darkness in his own eyes. Darkness he'd seen in the men who had beat him, the men who'd starved their own biological kids to pay for beer, the men who had hit their wives and terrorized their families. He'd once watched his first foster dad chain a seven-year-old girl in a doghouse for the night because she'd taken the change from the couch cushions to buy candy.

That night, as ten-year-old Blake had listened to his foster sister cry and beg for someone to come get her, he had vowed he would never hurt anyone the way he'd watched so many people be hurt. He'd sworn he would be the type of man who helped people, who made their lives better.

But now he was standing above a woman he'd forcibly bound to a bed, listening to her cry.

At that moment, something inside him snapped.

He had to stop this. Now.

Before he hurt Erin any more than he already had, and before he committed an act of violence that would haunt him forever.

CHAPTER TWO

Erin

"I'm sorry, Erin. Please, don't cry." Blake flipped off the tattoo machine and stripped his gloves off with two angry motions. "I don't know what's wrong with me. I never should have started this fucking crazy shit."

Erin felt him working to untie the ropes at her feet, but even knowing she was soon going to be free didn't help stop the tears. If anything, it made them worse. She was crying so hard her entire body ached and her chest felt like it would implode at any second.

The sobs echoing through the room didn't even sound like hers. She sounded like a wounded animal, a creature that had been caged for too long.

All the pain of the past three years, all the fear and anger and despair, hit like a physical blow. It was as if Blake's tattoo needle had torn a hole in her heart and everything she'd held inside was spilling out all at once.

"Please, babe. Please, I'm sorry," Blake whispered into her hair as he worked the key into the cuffs on her wrists. "I'm sorry."

Erin wanted to tell him it wasn't his fault, at least not all of it. His betrayal was the cherry on top of a shit sundae of hurt. She wanted to tell him that it was okay, that he'd stopped in time and she wasn't as angry as she'd been before. She wanted to say it wasn't the tattoo modification, but the lack of respect for her free will that had finally pushed her into a meltdown.

But she couldn't stop crying long enough to say anything.

So she did the only other thing that felt right. As soon as her arms were free, she rolled onto her back and reached for him, holding both arms out like Abby did when she wanted to be picked up. She was still crying and could feel her nose beginning to leak, but for once she didn't worry about what kind of face she was putting on for the man in her bed. She just needed Blake to know she cared about him, no matter how insane the past few hours had been. She just wanted him to hold her, to wrap her in his strong arms, and tell her everything was going to be okay, even if it was a lie.

"Erin." All he said was her name, but she saw the shine in his eyes before he pulled her close, crushing her against his chest.

He loved her. He really did.

The thought made her sob harder, more tears pouring out to soak his sweater.

God, this was so fucked up. Blake was insanely fixated on their matching tattoos, thought she was a criminal, had kidnapped her—twice—and was clearly as in need of serious therapy as she was, but…he loved her. Blake loved her: maybe madly, but truly, deeply. She could feel it every time they touched, in the way being close to him made her chest ache, mourning the loveless years she'd wasted with a man who thought of her as just another decoration for his Bel Air mansion.

Erin snuggled closer to Blake's chest, reveling in the foreign sensation of being home. The urge to cry slowly vanished in the wake of that warm, sheltered feeling, the feeling she always had when she was this close to Blake. He was the only man who had ever been able to turn her on and calm her down at the same time.

Even now, when he was the person she should be afraid of, his arms felt like the safest place in the world.

"I'm so sorry." He kissed the top her head, the tension in his voice making it clear how grueling he'd found her crying jag. Poor Blake, he'd never been able to handle seeing a woman cry. "I've obviously lost my damned mind. I never wanted to hurt you, sweetness, I never—"

"It's okay," she whispered, not wanting to lift her face from his chest.

"No, it's not okay," he insisted. "But I'm going to make it okay. We'll leave whenever you want. I'll take you home or to the police or wherever you want me to take you. I'm just…so sorry."

"I'm sorry, too," Erin said, hugging him closer. "This wasn't all your fault, you know. That had been building up for a long time. I mean, I've done my share of crying the past three years, but nothing like that."

Blake's muscles relaxed a bit and one hand began to smooth idly up and down her bare back. "Your marriage was that bad, huh?"

He reached over to the side of the bed and

17

plucked a Kleenex from the box. Erin took the tissue and did her best to mop up her face without moving too far from Blake. She needed to be close to him right now. It made her feel stronger for some reason.

"Yes, it was that bad." She sighed, amazed that thinking of Scott no longer summoned the familiar rush of hurt and rage. It was as if she'd finally cried him out of her system.

Now she just had to get him out of her life and she would truly be ready to move on.

Blake grunted. "You want to tell me about it?"

"Not really," she said. "I haven't told anyone. I've been too ashamed."

"I'm sure you have nothing to be ashamed of," he said, kissing the top of her head again, sending a wave of melancholy rushing through her.

"Oh, I do." Erin laughed, a short, sad sound. "I was really, really stupid. Crazy, fucked in the head, stupid."

"Hey, you're talking to the guy who

kidnapped his high school girlfriend." He smoothed her hair from her forehead. "You can't get much more fucked in the head than that."

This time her laugh was genuine.

Jesus. Only Blake could make her laugh a few minutes after crying her eyes out.

"So spill it," he said. "I'm not going to judge. I'm in no position to."

Erin took a deep breath, not certain how to begin. So she started with the basics, how she'd met Scott at one of the classier BDSM clubs in town. How he'd captured her interest from the start, seeming so much more Dominant than any of the other men she'd met. She told Blake how Scott had swept her away for long weekends at posh resorts up and down the California coast, and then surprised her with a giant rock four months into their relationship.

"We were married two months later, near Santa Barbara, at a winery," Erin said, feeling oddly detached from the story of her life. All of those happy memories seemed like they had happened so long ago, like they were the backstory for a different person than the woman she was now.

"Sounds like a fairy tale so far," Blake said. "If you're a submissive woman who's into really rich guys."

Erin smiled. "Yeah, it was pretty good. We had a great time together, and he was always respectful. Scott kept the Dom thing going just about all the time, but he never pushed my limits. I guess that's why I had no issue with signing the paperwork he had his lawyers draw up before the wedding. And I was twenty-one and stupid, that was a big part of it, too."

"A prenup agreement?" Blake asked.

"Well, there was that, but there was also a master-slave agreement." She lifted her head from his chest, glancing up at him through her lashes. "You ever heard of those?"

"I have." The dark note in his voice made it clear he didn't like the sound of them. "I don't know too many long-term Dom-sub couples, so I don't have any personal experience, but I've heard of them."

God, how she wished *she* didn't have any personal experience with them.

If she could go back in time and refuse to sign the thing, she'd do it in a heartbeat, even if it meant she had to relive those years with Scott. No matter how awful they'd been, her beautiful, sweet Abby had come out of that time, so Erin could never count them as a waste.

She sighed, not in a hurry to get to the next part of the story. "From what I understand, there isn't a standard boilerplate contract for the master-slave agreement. It's as open or restrictive as the Dom and sub decide for it to be."

Blake hummed beneath his breath, making his chest vibrate. "Let me guess, this guy wanted it as restrictive as he could get it."

Erin wet her lips. "Yep. I signed over control of almost everything. My money, my right to drive, to leave the house without Scott chaperoning—all kinds of things that should have rung alarm bells, but didn't." She squeezed her eyes shut. "Like I said. I was stupid."

"But those contracts aren't really legal, Erin," Blake said. "It's not like a Dom-sub agreement would stand up in court."

"Oh, I know," she said, bitterness creeping into her tone. "But that didn't matter once we were married. I had no money, no car to drive. No way out. Not that I wanted out, not then anyway. I started to get tired of the full-time control, but we were making it work."

Erin's jaw clenched. It was time to drop the big bomb. She knew it was though she feared what Blake would think of her when he discovered how she'd failed her child. "Things didn't get really bad until I accidentally got pregnant."

She risked a peek up into his dark eyes, but he didn't look surprised.

"You knew?" she asked, brow wrinkling in

confusion.

Blake nodded. Just once. "I had a friend check up on you while you were getting ready. He told me you had a one-year-old little girl. Abigail?"

"Abby, she'll be one in a few weeks," Erin said, anger spiking in her bloodstream as she remembered what she'd overhead. "And I heard you talking to your *friend*, trying to see if I had a criminal record."

She propped up on her arms, glaring at Blake. "What the hell, Blake? I've never done anything illegal, except get a tattoo when I was sixteen. I never even drank that much until I was twenty-one."

"Is that why you ran? Because you heard me on the phone?" He looked so hopeful Erin couldn't hold on to her anger.

She let out a long breath as she propped her chin on top of her fists. "It made me feel like you didn't trust me and that hurt so much. I mean, I'd given you my trust, even though you were the one who—"

"Abducted you and hauled you off to my mountain lair?"

She lifted a wry brow. "Yeah. That."

"I know. And I'm sorry. For all of it." Blake leaned close, kissing her on the lips for the first time since they'd fought. "Can you forgive me?"

Could she?

Of course she could. She was already halfway there.

The better question was: should she?

Should she let herself forgive Blake, even when he'd proven he was as crazy as she was?

CHAPTER THREE

Erin

Electricity swept over Erin's skin, tightening her nipples, making her keenly aware that she was almost naked in Blake's arms.

"Maybe," she said in a breathy voice, her gut telling her she'd never be able to hold a grudge against this man, no matter how hard she might try. "But it hurt, Blake. A lot."

"I understand, but I was only trying to

help," he said. "You said you had secrets and I wanted to make sure that, whatever those secrets were, I could still make things okay for us. I was trying to make sure I was in a position to protect you, Erin. That's all."

"Oh." When he put it like that, it was…sweet.

Controlling, but sweet.

Still, she wasn't up for another relationship like the one she'd had with Scott and Blake needed to get that message—right now. "But you should have trusted me to tell my secrets when I was ready," she said. "Not gone behind my back and violated my trust."

"I know. I'm sorry." He reached up, cupping her cheek tenderly in his hand. "And I should never have forced you to come back here with me. It was wrong."

"Well…don't let it happen again," Erin said, trying hard to resist the urge to claim his lips and kiss him until they both forgot all the mistakes they'd made. After years of celibacy, her libido still hadn't gotten enough of this man.

Celibacy.

Unfortunately, that brought her back to her story. She might as well finish the sad, stupid tale and get it over with.

"So, anyway," she said with a sigh. "I got pregnant with Abby and I was so, so excited. She wasn't planned, but I'd always wanted kids. I figured it was a happy surprise and expected Scott to feel the same."

Blake's eyes darkened. "But he didn't?"

"He tried to convince me to have an abortion." She swallowed against the familiar surge of loathing that rose inside her whenever she thought about her ex. "When I refused, he just…shut off. He barely spoke to me for weeks. He wouldn't touch me or sleep in the same bedroom and started staying at the office later every night. He said he found pregnancy repulsive."

"Son of a bitch," Blake growled.

Erin's lips twitched. "I think that was part of the problem. His mother is a real freak show and he was an only child. I think he equates women who are mothers with evil or something. At least that's the hypothesis I came to in my freshman psych class."

"You went to college?" he asked, obviously pleasantly surprised. "That's amazing, Erin."

What a difference from Scott, who had mocked her attempts to start school when she was already older than most of the graduating seniors. He'd insisted he made plenty of money and she was better off at home, serving her husband like a good submissive wife.

"Thanks. But I only did two semesters," she said, with a shrug. "One when I was pregnant with Abby and one after. They had a really good child-care room at the community college and it was close enough for me to walk there from our house, so…"

"That's great," he said. "You should go back and finish up. You were always good at school."

Her eyes began to tear again at the simple

compliment. Blake was the only man she'd ever known who seemed to value her brain as much as her body. Hell, the only one who even realized that she *had* a brain. Most guys got an eyeful of the blond hair and big boobs and didn't look much further.

"Oh, no, please don't cry. I'm not sure I can take much more." He laughed, but she still did her best to pull it together. She didn't want to cry anymore, either. Her head was already throbbing.

"So what happened after Abby was born?" he asked.

She rolled her eyes. "Scott didn't like my post-pregnancy body any more than my pregnant one, but that was fine by me. At that point, I was already looking for a way out."

She traced the pattern on Blake's sweater, concentrating on the swirls instead of her own words. "But Abby was so tiny and helpless and I was scared. I didn't know how I'd survive with a newborn, no job, and not a dime to run away on. And to be fair, Scott did seem to love Abby…in his way, once she outgrew the colic and started smiling and playing more."

"But that doesn't sound like a good life. For you or Abby."

"It wasn't," she said, stomach cramping as she remembered how alone she'd felt during those long, dark days. "And Scott made it obvious he resented the fact that I'd ruined his plans to never have children. At first he just ignored me, but then he started to say things."

"What kind of things?" Blake asked, anger simmering in his tone.

She shrugged. "Anything that would hurt. He'd talk about how my looks had gone downhill, how I was a lazy housewife—even though he had a maid come in twice a week so there wasn't much cleaning to do. He'd say I was a high school dropout too dumb to be trusted with a child or—"

"Where does he live?" Blake asked sharply. "Because I've suddenly got a strong desire to punch him in his ugly mouth."

"No! You can't. Promise me you'll never go near him." As soon as the panicked words were past her lips, Erin realized her response had been too strong, but it was too late.

"You're still afraid of him," Blake observed, eyes narrowing. "But you don't have to be, Erin. Not anymore. I swear I won't let that nasty fuck hurt you again."

Erin swallowed hard.

God, could she tell him? Would Blake help her, or would he think she was a piece of shit herself for letting Scott get his hands on her child?

"I promise you," Blake insisted. "No matter what happens with me and you, I'm going to make sure you're safe."

"It's not me I'm worried about," she said, rushing on before she could second-guess herself. "When I finally left him, I took Abby. I changed our names and tried my best to hide, but I didn't run far enough. He found us and he...took her."

Blake frowned. "Took her? How? You're both her parents, no court in California is going to—"

"We haven't gone to court and we probably won't," Erin said. "Scott had his lawyer draw up a divorce decree that he expects me to sign as is. It gives him full custody of Abby."

"That's bullshit," Blake said, his muscles tensing. "Your lawyer will fight that. There's no way that asshole can—"

"I don't have a lawyer."

"Then we'll get you one. Tomorrow. First thing." Blake paused, obviously waiting for her to respond, but she didn't know what to say. How to confess the worst of it. "Erin? Did you hear me?"

Blake captured her face in his hands, urging her to look up and meet his eyes. The confusion she read there made her chest ache. But then, he had every right to be confused. She hadn't told him the worst of it, the reason she was scared to death to lawyer up and fight for her baby girl.

"Scott is dangerous," Erin said, heart beating faster as she tried to finish this awful story. But for some reason, it was nearly impossible to bring herself to say the words. As if saying them out loud might make the danger to Abby more real.

"I understand why you're afraid," Blake said gently. "But you can't let this creep bully you out of your child's life. She needs you. You have to fight for her."

"Believe me, there's nothing I'd like more. I love Abby more than anything in the world. I promise you that." The back of her throat grew tight. "And I know living with Scott isn't a good situation for anyone, especially a baby."

"Then let's go get her," Blake said, the intense look in his eyes leaving no doubt he meant every word. "I'll drive you there tonight. We'll walk in and take Abby and I'll beat the living hell out of the man if he tries to get in our way."

Erin rolled her eyes again. "Great, Blake. And then he'll call the police and you'll be arrested and I'll look like an unfit mother for bringing my boyfriend to beat up my husband. This is not something that can be solved with fists. We're not in high school anymore."

Blake sighed. "You're right. I just can't stand to think of that man having your baby. I've got a bad feeling about it."

"You should." Erin swallowed past the lump in her throat. "Because Scott said he would kill Abby before he'd let me be a part of her life."

"What?" Blake's voice was thick with equal parts rage and disbelief.

Erin's pulse beat fast and thready in her throat. "If I fight for custody or try to take her again, he said he'd kill her. That he'd be careful and make sure no one would ever suspect that it was anything but an accident."

Blake looked stunned. "He wouldn't. He's bluffing to scare you."

"No, he's not, Blake." Her voice shook and she suddenly felt the chill lingering in the cabin. "If there's one thing I learned about Scott Sakapatatis in the years we were married it's that he always keeps his promises. Always. Especially the scary ones."

CHAPTER FOUR

Blake

Blake was quiet for a few minutes, his mind racing as he pulled a trembling Erin so close it felt like the fronts of their bodies would fuse together.

Not only was he a head case, he was a fool.

He should have known Erin would never lie and say she loved him just to gain her freedom. She wouldn't have reached for him after he set her free or be spilling her guts right now if she didn't love him. She wasn't the type to talk emotional stuff with anyone but her nearest and dearest, but her feelings were as real as the passion between them.

And as real as the hellish position she was in with her husband.

No wonder she'd let the bastard take their daughter. Even if the man were lying, what mother would be willing to risk the chance— even the slight chance—that he wasn't? He was threatening her child's life, for God's sake.

Scott was a fucking monster, whether he was bluffing with the death threat or not.

"I'm just spit-balling," Blake said in a low, soothing voice. "But couldn't you tell a DHS worker about what he said? Wouldn't that be enough to get Abby removed from his home?"

"DHS is overworked and underfunded and they call before they visit a home. You know that. I'm scared to risk it." Erin's breath rushed out on a shaky breath. "Besides, who would take my word over Scott's? I'm a high school dropout who worked as a lingerie model, and now I'm a bartender at a sleazy bar. He's a rich real estate investor who graduated top of his class at Stanford."

Blake wanted to tell her things like that wouldn't matter, but he knew better. Classism was still very alive and well, especially in California.

"Your silence is reassuring," she said, shifting in his arms, the way her breasts pressed against his chest reawakening his need for her. Even now, in the midst of this terrifying conversation, he still wanted to be inside Erin.

When they were making love, when he was buried to the hilt in her gripping heat, he didn't have to think about anything. Not the danger her little girl was in, not the uncertain future, and certainly not the fact that he wasn't the man he'd thought he was only a few short weeks ago. He'd not only followed through on his plan to kidnap Erin, he'd chased her down like an animal when she'd run and used brute force to haul her back to his cabin. He obviously wasn't right in the head and was displaying far more similar traits to her bully of an ex-husband than he wanted to admit.

Even if he figured out a way to help her and cleared the path for them to start dating, how could he be sure he was any better for her than the man he'd helped her escape? He'd never dream of threatening a child—the thought sickened him—but not so long ago he'd been certain he'd never kidnap a woman and tattoo her against her will, either…

Did he even know what he was capable of anymore?

"Blake? Is something wrong?" Erin's eyes were worried, but she still clung to him the same way she had since he'd untied her.

When she'd reached for him, offering him comfort in spite of what he'd done, Blake had thought his heart would explode. She really did care; it hadn't all been a lie.

But maybe she would have been better off if it had been.

He loved her, but who knew if love would be enough? Could Blake be certain he'd do any better by Erin than her ex? Sure, he'd never ignore her or tear her down with words, but who knew what else he'd do once he'd settled into being the Dominant man around the house. No matter how strong Erin was, she was a submissive. She would place her trust in him and have faith that he would make the best decisions for them both.

But what if he couldn't handle the responsibility for two lives—three including her daughter's? What if he wasn't the man he thought he was, and ended up bringing even more hurt into the life of the woman in his arms?

"I wish you'd talk to me," she whispered. "You're starting to freak me out."

Blake winced. He *should* freak her out. He'd been acting like a maniac since the night he headed out of Vegas, bound for California. "Sorry, I was just thinking."

"About what?"

"About how we can make sure Scott is the one considered an unfit parent," he said, the lie sliding easily from his lips.

He couldn't tell Erin about his doubts about himself. Not now, not when she obviously had no one else to turn to.

"My partner and I opted out of another season of *Vegas Ink*," he continued. "But I'm still in touch with a lot of the cameramen who used to work on the show. Most of them are based in L.A., so it shouldn't be hard to find someone willing to loan us equipment."

"What kind of equipment?" she asked, a hint of hope creeping into her voice.

"A hidden camera or two, a couple of microphones so tiny you can barely see them. A few things for a sting operation."

Her eyes lit up and Blake couldn't help but smile. "You think that could work?"

He nodded. "If we can get Scott on film

threatening Abby, any judge out there will give you a restraining order and full custody until you go to trial, at the very least. If we're lucky, the bastard might even get jail time."

"You really think so?" Erin asked, the excitement clear in her voice. "But we'd have to make sure Abby was safe before we showed anyone the film."

Blake thought for a moment. "I'll talk to my partner, Rafe. He used to be a cop. He should have some good advice on how to handle your ex."

"He has experience with domestic disputes as well as digging up private information on innocent people?" Erin narrowed her eyes, making it clear she didn't think much of Rafe. "I'm not sure I want this guy's help if it's all the same to you."

"Rafe's a good guy. I'm the jerk who was nosing around behind your back," he said, meaning it.

What had happened to the levelheaded man he'd always prided himself on being? It was like every ounce of restraint or common sense went out the window as soon as Erin was in the picture.

"But if you don't like him once you meet him, we'll go it alone," he added. "We probably won't need that much help anyway. Scott has to go to work and leave Abby alone sometime. Is she at a daycare center or——"

"He has a nanny. Two of them—a day nanny and a night nanny. But I still have the key to the house." She chewed her lip, obviously working through the scenario in her mind. "I'm sure he hasn't changed the locks or the code on the security system. He doesn't expect me to go against him in this."

"So we'll wait until Scott's out of the house and go in and take Abby," Blake said. "Since we'll have proof of Scott's threats by then, I doubt you'll catch any legal flak for doing whatever it takes to protect your little girl."

"And I know exactly when to do it!" She pushed into a seated position, treating Blake to a very distracting view of her breasts.

Erin noticed the direction of his stare, but didn't move to cover herself. Instead, she smiled, a secret little smile that made his cock even harder.

"There's this new BDSM club Scott was visiting pretty regularly before I left," she said. "It's out in the Valley, but a lot of the girls who go there don't mind swapping partners."

Erin's expression left no doubt how distasteful she found the practice. Good. Blake wasn't into sharing and had never understood Doms who got off on watching their submissive partner perform sexually with other men.

She chewed her lip. "We can stake out the club. Then, when he shows up, we head back to the house and get Abby. By then, she and the night nanny will probably be asleep, so we can just sneak in and out without anyone even knowing we were there."

"Sounds like a plan," Blake said, reaching for Erin in spite of himself.

With all the doubts still swirling in his

mind, the last thing he should be doing was making a move to continue their sexual relationship. They should be friends and nothing more until her little girl was safe and they'd had time to talk about what they wanted for the future.

But when Erin took his hands and pushed them above his head, straddling him with that naughty smile, he didn't try to fight her.

One glimpse of the heated look in her eyes and he was a goner.

CHAPTER FIVE

Blake

Erin leaned over him, teasing him with her breasts, brushing the soft skin against his face as she lifted first one of his wrists and then the other to the headboard. "Thank you. You don't know how much this means to me."

Blake didn't fight. He let her cuff him, figuring she deserved the chance to turn the tables after what he'd done. After he'd manhandled her and tied her down without permission.

The thought was nearly enough to make his cock soften, but then Erin was kissing him, pushing her tongue into his mouth, making him groan. She tasted so fucking sweet, like everything he'd hungered for his entire life. He met her strokes with his own, exploring every inch of her mouth.

By the time Erin pulled away with a quick nip at his lower lip, both of them were breathing faster. Seconds later she was busy at his belt buckle, tearing off his belt, fumbling with his fly, her hands shaking like she hadn't been laid in years.

"No foreplay?" he asked, groaning again as his swollen length sprung free.

Erin shoved his jeans and boxer briefs to his knees and then made quick work of her little black panties. "No foreplay. I want you inside me. Now."

She rose up over him in one smooth motion, spreading the lips of her sex and positioning his cock at her entrance. Seconds later he was inside her silken sheath, encased all the way to his aching balls.

"God, Erin." He moaned as she leaned forward, her hair spilling in silky waves around his face as she captured his lips once more.

They kissed for what seemed like forever, a slow, sensual meeting of lips, teeth, and tongue that communicated so much more than words. Less than a half hour ago, he'd thought he'd never know this kind of connection with Erin ever again. That sense of loss was still so close to the surface, intensifying the pleasure of every kiss, setting the places they touched on fire.

And slowly driving him even further out of his mind.

It didn't help that Erin limited her movement to tiny circles of her hips, grinding against him so only the base of his cock felt the friction of sliding in and out of her tight heat. The slight movement made him impossibly thicker, harder, until things low in his body cramped with an almost painful pleasure.

It was a sweet breed of torture, lying there beneath her. He was dying to buck his hips, to drive inside her, hard and fast. But he only hummed into her mouth, forcing himself to follow her lead, to let her set the pace.

"Blake." She breathed his name, the arousal clear in her voice making his jaw clench.

Damn, it was hell to hold back, to force his movements to mimic Erin's own. But he could feel how her pussy clenched each time he nudged against her clit. She was close to the edge, her muscles strung tight and her breath coming in swift, shallow bursts. The arms braced on either side of his face trembled and her hands fisted in the pillow beneath him. She only needed the slightest push and she'd shatter, her cunt clenching around his cock.

Thankfully he had just the perfect push in mind. "I want to suck my tits. Move for me."

Erin obeyed with a moan, shifting on top of him so that her breasts and her tightly puckered nipples were within easy reach. Blake's breath caught at the erotic beauty of her flushed skin. She was so perfect, the only woman who had ever literally taken his breath away.

He captured one rosy tip in his mouth, sucking and nibbling, tracing the pebbled flesh with his tongue until Erin writhed on top of him. She picked up the pace of her movements, more wet heat gushing from her sex as he transferred his attention to the other breast, dragging his teeth over her nipple before licking away the sting.

"Are you going to come for me?" he asked, in between flicks of his tongue. "Are you going to come on my cock?"

"Oh, God. Oh, God, yes." She moaned, the circling of her hips growing more and more frantic until finally she threw her head back with a wild cry. Her back arched, pressing her breasts closer to his face as she came.

Blake sucked harder, pulling at her sensitized flesh until she screamed his name and began to move again. In seconds, she was coming a second time, fingernails digging into his shoulders with enough force for it to sting, even through the thick fabric of his sweater. The feel of her slick, hot pussy clutching at him a second time was almost more than he could take.

"Fuck, Erin," he mumbled against her soft, damp skin. "Ride me. Ride me hard."

She sucked in a deep breath, braced her hands on his chest and lifted her hips, slamming them back down. She set a brutal rhythm, sheathing him inside her again and again. The sound of flesh slapping against flesh filled the room as her ass made impact with his thighs, underscored by the grunts and groans as each of them neared the edge. Blake arched to meet her as she dropped her hips, intensifying their connection, reaching all the way to the end of her and still not feeling as if he'd ever get close enough.

The smell of her arousal spun through his head, making his hands itch to reach between them, to gather some of the wet heat dampening her thighs and bring his fingers to his mouth. He wanted to taste her at the same time he lost himself inside her, wanted to drown himself in every aspect of Erin.

"Blake. God, Blake," she gasped, her rhythm starting to falter.

"Harder, faster. Don't stop." He watched her breasts bounce as she began to ride him once more. His swollen balls ached, throbbing with the need to come, but he forced himself to hold back his release, to savor every last moment of being inside his girl.

"I'm going to come, Blake. I can't, I—"

"Come," he groaned, the sound transforming to a cry of surrender as orgasm hit them both at the same moment.

His cock jerked inside of her even as her pussy clenched around him, milking every last drop of seed from his body. Things low in his body twisted in ways that didn't feel natural, but they sure as hell felt good. He couldn't remember ever coming so hard his vision blurred and his senses struggled to contain the pure pleasure exploding inside his every cell.

His ears were ringing by the time his body and soul finally reconnected, the blood pounding through his veins making him hard of hearing.

That was the only explanation as to why he didn't notice the men standing in the doorway to the bedroom until the taller one cleared his throat.

Blake blinked and his every muscle went rigid. "What the fuck are you doing in my house?" He sounded fucking dangerous, but he was cuffed to a bed and not in a position to be doing anyone damage. If these men wanted to hurt Erin, they wouldn't have to try very hard.

Blake mentally cursed himself for being so careless. He must have forgotten to lock the door. A stupid call out here in the middle of nowhere, where they had more than their share of backwoods crazies.

Erin let out a squeak of surprise and leapt off of him, burrowing under the covers before poking her head back out. "Oh my God, you scared the hell out of me," she said, breath coming fast as she flipped one edge of the blanket over Blake's now exposed cock. Still, she didn't sound afraid.

Probably because the men were cops.

After a second look at the door, Blake noticed the khaki uniforms and the holsters, complete with walkie-talkies and standard-issue firearms.

Shit. The people at the diner must have called the cops after all.

"We were just leaving, ma'am," the younger man said, tipping his hat and directing his eyes to a spot on the ceiling. "We'd gotten a report there might be a woman in trouble up here, but obviously we were mistaken."

"Unless you're the one in trouble, sir," the taller man asked, a shit-eating grin on his face, though he too had the decency to avert his eyes from the bed.

"Nope, no trouble." Blake willed his voice to stay calm and collected, to not betray the anxiety he felt. If Erin were going to turn him in, she would have done it already. Right? "At least not any trouble I don't want to be in."

"And you, ma'am? If you want to leave, we can wait while you get dressed and escort you back to town." The younger man's hand rested near where his gun was holstered, making it clear he was ready to do whatever it took to protect and serve.

"No, I'm fine. We were just having a little argument earlier. Disagreeing about wedding plans." She laughed, such a genuine sound Blake would never have guessed she was lying if he didn't know better. "You know how stressful weddings can be."

"I understand, but you had a few people worried." The older cop sighed but didn't seem overly annoyed. He and his partner probably hadn't had much else to do tonight in a community like this one. "Try to watch yourself more carefully in the future."

"Will do. Thanks, officers." Erin smiled and actually waved as the two men turned and tromped down the stairs.

Blake lay beside her, holding his breath until he heard the door slam below them.

That had been entirely too close. What if he hadn't stopped modifying Erin's tat in time? What if the policemen had entered the room to find a sobbing woman tied to his bed and him jabbing at her with a needle?

Getting arrested wouldn't have been anything he didn't deserve at that point, but still…

The enormity of his risk finally hit him full on. Rafe had been right. It had been a form of suicide to kidnap Erin. Even the fact that she had seemed happy to be with him most of the time they'd been together didn't make up for it. He was a madman, a criminal, and not nearly good enough for the woman giggling as she rolled over him to fetch the handcuff keys.

"Ohmygod, that was awful! I've never been caught in the act before. I nearly peed myself I was so scared." She unlocked the cuffs and then hurried into the bathroom, still laughing, calling over her shoulder as she ran, "I'm so embarrassed!"

Blake heard the water running and then the toilet flush, but not even those normal sounds could thaw the cold clutch of fear in his chest. He was going to have to watch himself very, very closely. Whatever madness had driven him to this point was probably still swirling around in his brain, waiting to come out and play. His job now was to make sure it didn't get the chance, that he never committed another criminal act around Erin or anyone else.

He'd help her, make sure she and her daughter were safe, and then he'd get the hell out of her life. It was the best thing he could do. There was no doubt he loved her, but she deserved a sane, rational man who would never think of doing half the things he'd done in the past two days.

Including taking sexual advantage of a woman in a vulnerable position.

"So, I'm starved. What about you?" Erin asked as she plucked her clothes from the floor and dressed. "Do you think that pasta you made is still good?"

"We can reheat it, and eat it on the road. Let's get everything packed up." Blake rolled from the bed and tugged his pants up around his waist.

"Okay," Erin said, her tone wary. "Are you all right?"

"I'm fine. I just think we should get back to L.A. The sooner we get things moving, the sooner we get your daughter back."

She nodded and walked toward her room, but stopped at the door to the bathroom and turned back to him. "I was never going to tell the police, Blake. Even if you'd forced me to change the tattoo, I wouldn't have. I care too much about you to do something like that."

Blake's heart lurched in his chest as he watched her disappear.

Her words only cemented his decision. He had to get out of her life, as soon as possible. He didn't deserve a woman like Erin.

He never had, and now he never would.

CHAPTER SIX

Three days later
Erin

"So we're all straight on where we need to be when?" Blake paced the luxury hotel suite where they'd been staying since their return to L.A. He'd thought it would be best if they stuck close to plan their strategy, which had been more than fine with Erin.

The suite was twice the size of her studio

apartment and she still couldn't get enough of Blake. Even after the sex marathon they'd had at the cabin, she'd been eager to get back between the sheets with the man. Making love to him was swiftly becoming an addiction.

Too bad he didn't feel the same way...

He hadn't touched her in three days. Instead of joining her in bed, he'd sacked out on the couch, leaving her one of the suite's bedrooms and his partner, Rafe, who had flown in from Miami, the other. Something was obviously bothering him, but she hadn't had the chance to talk to him about it. Rafe or one of his other friends always seemed to be around. They hadn't had ten minutes alone together since the ride back to L.A.

But if she were honest with herself, she'd felt him pulling away even then. Ever since their brief and embarrassing encounter with the police, he'd been acting differently. He was still committed to helping her get her daughter back, but he didn't seem interested in continuing what they'd begun up at the cabin.

Erin knew she shouldn't let that hurt her so much. Two days was nothing in the scheme of things, and saying you loved someone didn't necessarily mean you were ready to try to make a relationship work. Hell, she wasn't even sure *she* was ready. She only knew she missed the connection they'd had, missed it so much it made her feel hollow inside.

But she had to pull herself together. Blake had his own life, his own plans for the future, and they had nothing to do with her. She should just be grateful he was using his connections to help her get Abby back.

And she was. But she was also disappointed. Profoundly.

For a moment or two there, she'd actually let herself believe that the future might hold something beautiful for her and the only man she would ever love.

"Rafe," Blake said, turning back to his friend, "do you remember where you're supposed to wait for the call?"

"Blake, we've been over it a hundred times." Rafe reached for the television remote, sinking farther down into the overstuffed couch. "Let's check out what's on pay-per-view and relax for a couple of hours, man."

His blasé attitude bugged Erin. A lot. This was her daughter's life on the line, after all. "If you don't want to help out with this," she said in a cool voice, "I totally understand. We can change the plan. Blake and I can do the bit at the club and then—"

"Of course I want to help, and I'm your man for breaking and entering. Believe me," Rafe said, turning his attention back to where Erin and the two cameramen sat at the mahogany dining table.

The monstrosity was bigger than her bed back at her studio apartment and reminded her way too much of the ostentatious furnishings in her former home. Scott had picked out all their pieces himself and his tastes ran to the large and overly embellished.

Just another thing they hadn't had in common. Erin had felt more at home in Blake's cabin after two days than she had in three years of wandering around Scott's garish showplace.

"This isn't breaking and entering," Erin said. "I have a key and the code to the security system."

"And what if the code has changed? What would you do then?"

"I don't know," she said, trying to keep anger from her tone. The man wasn't trying to be argumentative, but he rubbed her the wrong way. "I'd figure something out."

"Figure something out. Good plan." He snorted, a derisive sound that made her grit her teeth.

Maybe the bastard *was* trying to be argumentative. Fine with her.

"Well, what are you going to do if Abby starts crying and wakes up the nanny?" Erin asked. "She doesn't know you, and I'm betting she's not going to like you very much."

"I'll have you know I'm good with ladies of all ages," Rafe said, that smirk on his face she knew most women would find sexy, but only made her want to strangle him. "You want references? I'm sure Blake would be willing to testify to my many successes with the fairer sex."

"Rafe." Blake's tone was a warning to cut the crap.

He was right. They didn't have time to argue.

Erin sighed, her anger flooding away as the cold reality of what they were planning set in once more. She was placing way too much trust in a man she didn't really know, and it scared her.

"Listen, I'm grateful for your offer to help," she said in a softer voice, "but I honestly think it would be better if I went."

Rafe met her eyes, the hard look on his face softening for one of the first times since she'd met him on Sunday. She'd been surprised to find Rafe fairly hostile, but had tried not to take it personally. She wasn't here to make friends. She was here to get Abby back.

"I grew up helping out with six little brothers and sisters," Rafe said, rising and coming to lean on the back of the empty chair across from her. "I'm good with kids, and if Abby is like most babies she sleeps like the dead once she's down. Am I right?"

Erin bit her lip, not wanting to admit he had a point. Whenever Abby fell asleep in her car seat, Erin had to move heaven and earth to get her awake enough to sit up in the buggy when they went grocery shopping. It had driven Scott so crazy she'd started riding in the backseat so she could play with Abby while they drove, keeping her awake until they reached the store.

"See. I know a few things about kids," Rafe said with a smile. "And I promise you, I'll have your baby here by the time you crazy kids get back from your kinky time."

"Speaking of, I'd like you dressed in about

an hour." Steve, the sound guy Blake had convinced to help them, reached for another slice of pizza.

He'd been eating nonstop since he arrived at the hotel room three hours ago and showed no signs of slowing down. It was obvious he came by his impressive bulk honestly. With his thick brown beard, friendly face, and giant belly, he resembled a twenty-something Santa Claus.

If Santa was a big porn fan.

Steve had grilled Erin for over an hour for all the details on the former porn stars she worked with at The Hard Way, keeping at it until she'd fled to the balcony pleading a need for fresh air. She wasn't a prude by any means, but porn wasn't really her thing.

Why spend hours watching badly staged sexual scenarios that catered to the male of the species, when you could actually be having sex?

Or maybe even making love, sharing more than a bodily connection with another person.

The way she and Blake did when they—

Not going there, remember?

Erin blinked away the mental images inspired by thoughts of her and Blake making love. "Do you want both of us dressed or just me?"

"Both of you. It could be tricky making sure the mics don't show in tight clothing," Steve said around a mouth full of pepperoni and olives. "It's going to be tight, right? I can't wait to see Blake in some second-skin leather pants."

"Thanks, Steve," Blake said dryly. "Though I have to confess, I didn't realize you swung that way."

"Only for you, Blake. Only for you." Steve batted his eyes and all the men laughed. Even Ken, the rather quiet Asian man in charge of the cameras, chuckled into his giant mug of coffee.

Erin probably would have laughed, too, if she weren't so nervous.

"I think I'll go ahead and shower and get

dressed now," she said, taking her coffee mug to the sink and dumping the last of the contents down the drain. She was already hyped up enough, the last thing she needed was more caffeine.

"Me, too. I'll use Rafe's bathroom." Blake shot her a reassuring smile as they crossed paths. Erin smiled back, trying not to think about how much more she'd enjoy the process of getting clean if they were to share a shower. She could use a little stress-relieving quickie right about now.

Who was she kidding? She could always go for a quickie if Blake were the man in question. She craved his hands on her, his voice whispering in her ear, telling her how to please him, taking away all fear and doubt. She really was hopeless, head over heels for another Dominant man before she'd even started divorce proceedings with the first man who'd taken control of her life.

Maybe *that* was why Blake didn't want her anymore. He'd seen how weak she was and wanted no part of it. He'd said a submissive's role required a lot more strength than a Dom's.

Maybe he'd decided she didn't have what it took to be his girl.

So what? If that's what he's decided, it's his loss.

Erin froze in the doorway to what had been her bedroom for the past few nights, shocked to her core. How long had it been since she'd felt enough pride in herself to assume anyone would be better off with her than without her?

Years. At least two.

A part of her knew she had Blake to thank for that, too. If he hadn't made her feel so intensely desired, who knows how long it could have taken to recover her lost confidence? The guys at The Hard Way had made it clear her body was still plenty interesting, but it was Blake who had made the person inside the body begin to feel whole again. She owed him for that, no matter what craziness had driven him to kidnap her in the first place.

So if he wanted out of what they'd started without a bunch of drama, she'd just have to do her best to let him go.

CHAPTER SEVEN

Erin

Erin sighed as she turned on the shower, ignoring the aching in her chest and the tightness at the back of her throat. She couldn't let herself dwell on the likelihood of losing Blake. There was too much riding on her ability to pretend they were a happy BDSM couple.

With the help of one of Rafe's many

mysterious connections, they'd scored a copy of the guest list and a pair of tickets for a special scene being held at Under My Thumb, the club in the Valley Scott had been frequenting before they split. Scott Sakapatatis was on the VIP list for the "Knights in Black Leather, Ladies in White Lace" costume event.

The knowledge made her shudder.

Barring some unforeseen change of plans, she'd be seeing her husband in a few hours. But this time she wouldn't be alone. She'd be accompanied by her new Dom, a man determined to help her get custody of her daughter. Though they weren't going to let Scott in on that fact right away.

The plan was for her and Blake to engage in some public play, doing their best to capture Scott's attention and hopefully inspire some old-fashioned jealousy, a tactic Erin was cautiously optimistic would work. Scott had found her undesirable for the past couple of years, but that didn't mean he was ready to see her serving another man.

After all, *she* was the one who'd left *him* and she knew that stung. Above all else, Scott craved control of the people in his life. The day he'd tracked her down at her new apartment, that craving had led to an offer to take her back. It was only after she refused that he'd lost it and snatched Abby from her crib.

Hopefully, he'd get nice and angry when he saw Erin letting Blake do so many of the things she'd never wanted Scott to do to her in public. Because the angrier he was, the more likely he would be to incriminate himself. On the chance the threats he'd made had been a heat-of-the-moment thing, they needed him heated tonight.

Then, once his temper was boiling, she'd fan the flames by asking him to step outside for a talk. A talk in which she'd tell him all about her new knight in shining armor and do her damnedest to get any threats he made on tape.

Once that was accomplished, the men monitoring the camera and sound feeds from a nearby van would call Rafe and give him the go signal. He'd be on the move from his location near Scott's house a few minutes later. Even if Scott left the club right after his chat with Erin, Rafe would still have plenty of time to get in, get Abby, and get out before Scott arrived home.

They'd decided it was too risky to wait and go after Abby a night or two after Erin and Blake's appearance at the club. Scott would be on his guard and suspecting something from his soon-to-be ex. If he hadn't changed the locks and security code previously, he would be much more inclined to then, and that would make gaining access to the home that much trickier.

This was the best plan they could come up with and it seemed to be a good one.

"Then why are you so nervous?" Erin asked her reflection in the steamy mirror as she stripped out of her white tee shirt and jeans.

Was it the chance of failure? The fear that she wouldn't really be holding Abby by the end of the night? Was it anxiety over seeing Scott for the first time in weeks?

Or maybe it was the way her heart rate accelerated when she looked at the white, nearly see-through peek-a-boo chemise and matching frilly shorts she'd be wearing in front of an entire room full of people tonight.

The outfit hung on the rod near the hotel towels, taunting her.

Even in her club days, she'd never been the type to go to a scene so scantily dressed. Leather shorts and a tank top with thigh-high boots had been more her style. She'd feel naked in the outfit Blake had picked out for her. And even more exposed because *he* had been the one to choose the ensemble. It was obviously the kind of thing he would have wanted his girl to wear.

Tonight she would be his girl.

He would finally touch her, tease her,

dominate her, for what might very well be the last time. And he'd do it all in front of a room full of people.

Public displays weren't her breed of kink, but Erin vowed she was going to make the most of the coming hours with Blake. Nerves be damned. She wasn't going to let her last chance to be mastered by Blake slip through her fingers. She had to put on a good show for Abby's sake, and she needed to feel Blake's strong hands upon her for her own. She needed the chance to say good-bye with more than words, to have one last kiss, one more chance to bask in the bliss of pleasuring the man she loved.

God, she loved him. It hadn't been some madness inspired by their crazy weekend. The feeling was still there now, simmering inside of her, growing stronger every day.

"Erin?" Blake's voice at the door made her jump and her heart race a little faster.

What was he doing here? Had he decided a team shower made more sense as well?

Before she could second-guess herself, Erin turned to the door, not bothering to cover her body with a towel. She was still wearing her bra and panties, and it wasn't like Blake hadn't seen everything she had to offer.

"Hey. What's up?" She opened the door, breath catching to see Blake standing in front of her wearing nothing but his faded black jeans.

His massive chest was bare, every muscle sharply delineated from his morning workout at the hotel gym. It was hell to resist the urge to lean forward and trace the lines of his six-pack with her tongue. She wanted to taste the light salt of his skin, wanted to kiss her way down his strong stomach while her fingers worked the close of his jeans.

It felt like ages since he'd had his hand fisted in her hair and his cock down her throat. She wanted to feel his hot, steely length shoving between her lips again, wanted to—

"Um, Ken said…" Blake's voice trailed off,

his breath rushing out between his parted lips.

His dark gaze met hers and Erin had no doubt he knew exactly what she'd been thinking. He swallowed hard, his eyes drifting down to take in her simple white bra and cotton panties. They weren't nearly as scandalous as what she'd be wearing tonight, but apparently Blake found them plenty interesting.

Erin smiled as she watched the crotch of his jeans grow tighter. "Ken said?"

"He said to make sure to wear your hair up," Blake said, his eyes lingering on her breasts until Erin's nipples pulled tight inside her bra. God, he could make her ache with just a look, make her pussy slick without laying a hand on her. "The cameras are hidden in the earrings he brought, and he doesn't want your hair getting in the way."

"Okay. Not a problem." She stood in the doorway, unmoving, wondering if she should risk making the first move. "Is there anything else?"

"No. Nothing else." He shook his head and stepped back, his gaze dropping to the floor.

Erin's heart sank in spite of herself. They were going to be together in a couple of hours; she should just suck it up.

But in a couple of hours they were going to be putting on a show for Scott. She wanted Blake to touch her before the pretense, to let her know he still felt something for her. Even if it was only lust.

"Blake, I—"

He was gone before she could finish her sentence, fleeing from the bedroom like his hair was on fire. That was how desperate he was to get away from her. His cock might still respond to the sight of her nearly naked body, but that was the end of it.

Blake didn't want her anymore. It was as if he'd forgotten the passion that burned so hot between them a few short days ago.

"Then I'll just have to make sure he remembers," Erin whispered as she closed the door and flung her bra and underwear onto the floor.

She stepped into the shower, determined to scrub, soap, shave, and loofah herself into a state of unparalleled desirability. She'd show Blake what he was missing and give him a night he'd never forget.

She might not be able to change his heart, but at least she could make sure she would haunt his mind. Blake would never enter another BDSM club again without thinking of what they'd done together.

She was going to make sure of it.

CHAPTER EIGHT

Blake

Under My Thumb was classier than Blake had anticipated. Compared to many of the clubs he'd frequented in Vegas, the joint was downright restrained.

Thick, gold and brown fabric wallpaper covered the walls of the main room, muting the soft rumble of conversation and lending a warm, cozy feel to the lounge area. Dozens of low tables and thickly padded black and gold chairs surrounded the circular bar at the center of the room, and a waterfall on one wall all but eclipsed the music coming from the play areas with the soothing sound of water tumbling over rocks.

If it weren't for the glimpses of bondage equipment and spanking tables in the darker rooms to his right and left, and the scantily clad submissive chained to a revolving platform above the bar, he and Erin could have been in any posh L.A. bar.

Well, any bar that allowed its patrons to bring their dates in on leashes.

A few feet ahead of them, half a dozen collared women and a couple of collared men knelt on the floor next to their Dominant partners' chairs, eyes downcast and secretive smiles on their faces. The sight put Blake's mind at ease about the personality of the club itself.

Safe, sane, and consensual seemed to be the rule. The patrons looked laid-back and relaxed, unconcerned for their own safety or anyone else's.

In fact, many of the couples were laughing and chatting, the subs fetching plates from the hors d'oeuvres table and the Dominants feeding their partners while they knelt at their feet. There was a loving feeling in the main room, and Blake knew he would have genuinely enjoyed spending a night here playing with Erin if they weren't here to confront her ex.

"Looks like I'm missing an important accessory," Erin whispered, glancing at the rhinestone-inlaid collar of a young blond sub as they made their way to the bar.

"Do you think I should have found you a collar?" Blake leaned down and breathed the words against Erin's neck, relishing the clean smell of her.

She looked so beautiful with her hair up, her neck long and graceful. He could amuse himself for at least half an hour just letting his lips play up and down that smooth column of soft flesh.

"There's a woman selling gear at one of the tables in the corner." Erin angled her body closer to his, the tips of her breasts brushing against his arm as he ordered them each a snifter of brandy. "I could follow you around on my hands and knees if you'd prefer."

"I don't need a collar to feel in control." Blake glanced down at her, catching the faintest glimpse of her berry-colored nipples through the white fabric of her lacy top.

It had been driving him wild since the second she stepped out of the bathroom and every male jaw in the hotel room had dropped to the floor. Even Rafe, who had done his best to make his dislike for Erin known, had gotten that wolfish look in his eyes. Like he wanted to pounce on Erin and devour her whole.

It had been all Blake could do to keep from teaching them all a lesson about where to keep their eyes when it came to Erin—on her face, nowhere else. Friends or not, he couldn't stand to see anyone else look at her with desire.

She was *his*, and no other man should touch her, not even with their eyes.

No, she's not yours, asshole. She deserves a better man and you're going to make sure she's free to find him, remember?

Blake paid the bartender and took a deep pull on his brandy, wincing as the liquid burned a trail down his throat.

He'd seen the way Erin had been looking at him since they'd returned to L.A. She wanted to pick up where they'd left off at the cabin. He did, too, but it wasn't what was best for either of them. He needed to get his head on straight and she needed the chance to meet a man who wouldn't do crazy things like kidnap her and try to tattoo her against her will.

He and Erin couldn't have that second chance he craved with every cell in his body. But they could have tonight.

One last night to last a lifetime.

"All right. But it looks like she's selling

whips, too." Erin sipped her drink as she traced a trail from his stomach to his chest with her fingertips, making him shiver. Even through the thick leather of his sleeveless shirt, he could feel the heat of her touch. "Are you going to spank me in front of everyone? Is that why the legs on these shorts are so loose?"

"Maybe." Blake's hand tightened reflexively on Erin's hip. He wanted nothing more than to find a bench and make her fantasy a reality, but they needed to take stock of their surroundings before they chose a place to play.

His next words were softer than a whisper. "Do you see him anywhere?"

Erin's wicked smile faltered. "No. Not in here. But he might be in one of the playrooms."

"Then let's take a tour." Blake tossed back the last of his drink and put a hand on the small of Erin's back, leading her into the room on their right.

Eyes followed them as they walked, but he wasn't surprised. Erin was easily the most gorgeous woman in the room, and he wasn't ignorant of the effect his own imposing bulk had on the average submissive. Together, they were the poster children for every BDSM fantasy—the delicate sub and the large muscled Dom.

They were going to have their share of observers once they settled in to play; there was no doubt about that. It wasn't the way Blake would have preferred to spend their last night together, but drawing attention was what they were trying to do tonight. If every tongue in the club was wagging about the new kids in town, there was no way Erin's husband could miss them.

"He's not here," she whispered.

It wasn't a big surprise—there were only four couples active in the large playroom at the moment—but Blake still felt his spirits sink.

What if Scott had decided not to come?

Blake wasn't in any hurry to see the sociopath who'd made Erin's life a living hell, but after all their planning, it would be infuriating if Scott didn't show. And Erin would be devastated. She was so thrilled by the thought of seeing her daughter again.

Blake was excited, too. He couldn't wait to meet the little blonde, brown-eyed girl he'd seen in Erin's pictures. Abby was the spitting image of her mom, a fact that made him love her before he'd even met her.

Fuck…he was hopeless where this woman was concerned. And probably the world's sappiest Dom. If Erin knew half the thoughts running through his head, his "big and bad" rep would be out the window in seconds.

"Nope, no Scott, but I like that big bench in the corner." She ran her tongue lightly over her lips. "I mean really, *really* like it."

"It's called a Black Stallion," Blake said, letting his hand wander down to cup Erin's ass through the soft satin of her shorts as he leaned down to murmur his next words into her ear. "They're made to support a lot of weight. I could position you at one end, spank you until your pussy is dripping down your thighs, and then climb up and fuck you from behind. It would support both of us."

Erin's breath came faster, her breasts rising and falling in a way that made Blake ache to get her tits in his mouth. "You think the boys in the van heard that?"

"No. I haven't switched the mics on yet. The power switch is built into my watch." His fingers teased under the hem of her shorts, tracing the curve of her ass, making her shiver. "I don't want any of them hearing or seeing anything but what they need to hear and see. Tonight, you're mine."

"Yes." Her eyes slid closed and her lips parted, an invitation Blake couldn't resist.

He captured her mouth with his, slipping his tongue between her lips, tasting the brandy she'd sipped and a sweeter, spicier taste that was pure Erin. As his tongue sparred with hers in an erotic dance, his fingers dipped between her legs. Pulling the scrap of fabric masquerading as her panties aside, he plunged first one finger and then a second into the molten heat of her pussy.

"God, you're so wet already, Erin," he said, his own breath coming faster.

"Wet and ready," she whispered, contracting her inner muscles until they gripped his fingers. "And dying to get fucked."

Blake kissed her again, moaning against her lips as his cock thickened within the tight confines of his leather pants.

God. Damn. How had he managed to go nearly three days without touching her? How had he resisted the overwhelming need to get his fingers, his mouth, his cock inside her sweet little pussy?

"Are you going to fuck me, Blake?" she asked, her breath coming faster as her hands molded to his chest. "Are you going to take me in front of all these people? Show them I'm yours?"

"We agreed, no penetrative sex, Erin. I'm not going to change my mind about that. But I will make sure you're satisfied." His drove his fingers in and out of her pussy one last time, making her eyelids flutter and her breath rush out on a moan. "But only if you're good."

Erin moaned as he pulled his hand from between her legs and brought his fingers to his lips. Holding her eyes, he sucked the two that had been inside her into his mouth, licking the taste of her from his skin.

Erin's nipples tightened until they poked through the thin fabric of her top. "Want me to show you how good I can be?" She licked her lips again, making it impossible not to think of that night at the cabin, when she'd sucked him off like she couldn't get enough of his cock.

"Soon. But not yet." With no small degree of effort, Blake forced his mind back to the business at hand. "Let's check out the other room," he said, running his knuckles over her nipples through the gauzy material as he spoke. "Then we'll find a place to play for a while."

"Yes, sir." Erin's words were perfectly submissive, but the look she cast up at him through her lashes was tinged with defiance. That look made it clear she wanted more out of tonight than a confrontation with her ex, that she wanted Blake to stake a claim.

He turned back to her, nearly encircling her narrow waist with his hands and squeezing. "I'm going to spank you, Erin. And bind you and make you scream my name when you come while these people watch. Don't doubt that for a minute."

Erin's hands drifted up to cling to his biceps, but he stopped her with a word. "Hands at your sides. Keep your hands to yourself until I tell you otherwise. Show me you can be patient."

"You know patience isn't one of my virtues." She narrowed her eyes, clearly not thrilled with the idea of waiting much longer.

"Give me another look like that one and you'll be punished."

"How would you punish me?" she asked, the arousal in her voice enough to make his cock twitch. She knew how to play him, how to dance the edge between obedience and defiance, ramping up his own desire.

"I think nipple torture would be most fitting," he said, smoothing his hands up to capture her tits in his palms. He pinched her nipples between his fingers as he continued to speak in the same low, soothing voice. "First I'll touch you like this until you squirm and your pussy drenches those little panties."

Erin sucked in a ragged breath but didn't say a word.

"Then, I'd find some nipple clamps. Or, in a classy joint like this, they might have dual electrode attachments for breast play. Have you ever had electricity shooting across your nipples, Erin?"

"I heard that could be dangerous. That it could cause a heart attack," she said, her hands fisting at her sides as she fought to hold still despite the fact that he'd intensified his attention to her nipples, rolling them in firm circles.

"Above-the-waist electrical play can be completely safe. As long as you know how to do it the right way."

"And I bet you know how to do it the right way, don't you?" Erin's words ended in a gasp as he pinched her nipples—hard—one last time and then pulled away.

"Of course I do." He smiled down at her, knowing he was walking a dangerous line by demanding a true power exchange from Erin.

It might be their last night together, but they had to make their relationship look like the real thing. But even if they weren't undercover, he couldn't seem to treat Erin any other way. He wanted to treat her the way he would if she were really his submissive, his girl, and they were learning how to be a Dom-sub couple for life.

The thought filled him with a longing so

fierce he felt like a jolt of electricity had surged into his heart.

"Let's check out the other room." He took her hand in his and walked toward the hall connecting the two playrooms.

The passageway was constructed so it appeared to be carved through solid rock and took patrons behind the waterfall located in the main lounge. There were several nooks and crannies along the way, perfect for a couple looking to hide in the shadows, but he and Erin were the only ones in the darkened tunnel.

It was only nine thirty and most of the clientele still seemed to be in the drinking, snacking, and chatting phase. If Under My Thumb were anything like other clubs he'd been to, the real action wouldn't start up until closer to midnight.

"Look, the backside of water," Erin said, laughing softly. "I always wondered what that looked like."

"You're the goofiest sex symbol I've ever

met." Blake smiled at her over his shoulder.

"I know." She laughed again as she turned back to look at the waterfall. "My jokes are horrible, I just can't..." She trailed off, her hand going slack in his, and the stricken look on her face making his heart race.

"What's wrong?" Blake pulled her close, senses on high alert. There was little doubt who had inspired the fear and anxiety in Erin's eyes. "It's him, isn't it?"

"Yes. He's sitting at the bar." Her voice was little more than a whisper.

She suddenly sounded so much younger and more unsure than the Erin who had sassed him in the other room or joked with him a few seconds ago.

And the bastard in the other room was responsible. He was the one who had done his best to break her spirit and it made Blake wish more than ever that he could get away with breaking the other man's face.

CHAPTER NINE

Blake

Blake moved behind Erin, banding his arms around her as he pulled her back against his front. He dropped a soft kiss on top of her head before he spoke. "Which one?"

"The one in the long-sleeved black shirt," she said, voice still trembling. "With the sandy blond hair."

Blake didn't know what he'd expected, but

the man seated a dozen feet away wasn't it.

Scott was amazingly…average-looking. Probably around five feet nine, average weight, average build, average Californian tan and light brown hair. Even an average-looking profile with a slight bump on the bridge of his nose. The only thing unique about the man was that he was sitting with a gorgeous, if rather artificial-looking, blonde with enormous breasts, wearing a white slip so transparent it made Erin's look modest in comparison.

"He's with someone. I should have known he'd be with someone," Erin said, nibbling her bottom lip. It was a nervous habit she'd had since she was a teen, and reminded him that—no matter how average-looking—this was a man capable of inspiring extreme anxiety in the woman he loved. "What if this doesn't work the way we planned, Blake? What if I can't get him alone?"

"Don't worry." Blake hugged tighter, willing his strength into her slim body. "Just because he's here with someone else doesn't mean he won't be pissed to see you here with another man. Besides, that woman has nothing on you. She's an imitation, you're the real thing."

She laughed, but it was no longer a carefree sound. "Scott likes imitation. He kept trying to convince me to get implants and a tummy tuck after Abby was born."

"He's certifiable," Blake growled. "You're perfect."

"Scott didn't think so. He saw every line, every stretch mark." Her hands trembled as they moved to grip his forearms, her fingers squeezing gently before abruptly dropping back to her sides. "Sorry, I forgot I wasn't supposed to touch you."

"Don't worry about it, sweetness," Blake said, feeling like an ass for putting more pressure on Erin.

She didn't need to be worried about obeying Dom-sub rules when she was getting ready to confront the man who had threatened her daughter's life.

"No, I *want* to worry about it." She turned in his arms and lifted her troubled eyes to his. "I need you, Blake."

"I'm here. Anything you need," he promised. "And I'll be close by when you ask him to go outside. No one is going to hurt you tonight."

"No, it's not that." She sucked in a deep breath. "I mean, don't back down, or take it easy on me. Make me yours."

"Erin, I—"

"Please?" She smiled, a sad twist of the lips. "Even if it's just for tonight."

So she knew. She could sense that this was the end. "Are you sure?" he asked, brushing a stray curl from her sinfully soft cheek.

"I've never been more sure of anything." The eyes that met his were filled with a longing so intense, Blake felt like he'd been sucker punched in the gut.

"Make me forget he's here," she whispered. "Make me forget that he might be watching.

Make me forget about everything but you."

CHAPTER TEN

Erin

Erin could barely breathe as she followed Blake back to the spanking bench she'd had her eye on earlier. Her mouth went dry and her lips buzzed. Her body felt numb except for the place where Blake's hand squeezed hers, and she figured there was a decent chance she was going to pass out.

She couldn't do this. Not really. She'd been

a fool to think anything about this night would be bearable, let alone enjoyable.

Scott was in the other room. If he swiveled around on his bar stool, he'd be able to see her without even leaving the lounge. There was no way she'd be able to concentrate on obeying Blake, let alone enjoy what he was going to do to her. Not knowing her ex could be watching.

What had seemed like such a fantastic idea in theory was proving very disturbing in real life.

She already felt violated by Scott in so many ways. Now she wanted to add this to the list? Let him watch while she submitted to another man, the very thing he'd always wanted her to do when they were first together? No matter how much she'd wanted to please him back in the early days, she'd never been able to bring herself to do as he asked.

She was a one-man girl, always had been. Once she fell for a guy, she didn't find any other male sexually attractive. And she couldn't let a man she wasn't attracted to touch her, not even to please the man she loved. The idea made her skin crawl, and reminded her of those nights back in Carson City, when Blake and Phil's wife wouldn't be home from work until late, when she was alone with Phil and the younger kids.

Her foster father's "attentions" hadn't crossed the line until she was almost sixteen, and she'd always managed to escape anything worse than a little inappropriate fondling, but she'd known it was only a matter of time before his advances escalated. That's why she'd run the morning after Blake left the house for good. It was either get out or put out; there'd been no doubt in her mind.

And there was no *way* she could have told Blake the truth about Phil. He would have gone crazy and gotten himself thrown in jail or worse. Besides, she'd been ashamed to tell him Phil sometimes had his hands on her only hours after she and Blake had been together.

It made her feel dirty, as if she were the one who had done something wrong.

Even years later, grown up and with psychology courses under her belt that should have taught her otherwise, she still felt shame every time she thought of those last nights in her foster father's home.

With thoughts of Scott and Phil floating around in her head, there was no way she'd be able to get turned on.

This just wasn't going to work.

"Blake, wait." She tugged on the hand he held, but he didn't slow his stride. "Maybe I should just go talk to him and forget about this. If I tell him I'm with someone else, I'm sure he'll—"

"Quiet, don't speak again until I give you permission." The command was thrown over his shoulder, but Erin could hear the determination in his tone loud and clear. She'd told him she wanted him to dominate her, and he'd taken her at her word.

There was no turning back now.

The knowledge awakened a thread of heat low in her body. She wasn't nearly ready to mount the bench Blake now circled with a critical glare, but neither did she want to vomit at the thought. Blake had banished her panic with a single sentence. It just went to prove what she'd been thinking since they left the cabin—he was the only man she wanted to top her, for now, for always.

Too bad he only wanted a one-night stand.

"Climb up," Blake ordered in his low, silky Dom voice, staring at her over the rounded leather hump of the spanking bench.

It looked almost like one of the pommel horses gymnasts vaulted over but with a ledge on either side to support the knees. In a few minutes, she could be straddling the thing, her ass presented for Blake's disciplining pleasure. The very thought made her pussy plump inside her panties, no matter how many reservations she still had.

Blake's eyes glittered. "Don't make me ask a second time."

Erin's breath rushed out as she darted a quick look into the lounge. Scott was still at the bar, and still had his back to them. Thank God.

"Look at me." Erin obeyed, gazing up at Blake, feeling her awareness of the outside world fade a bit as their eyes connected. "Don't look at him, don't think about him. He's not here. There's no one else here. No one but you and me. Do you understand?"

Erin nodded, her nipples drawing tight against the thin fabric of her shirt. Just the sound of Blake's voice, so deep it vibrated against her skin, was enough to turn her on. The electricity that never failed to make an appearance when they were together arced between them, making her breath come faster and her hands itch.

She wanted to feel him, to run her fingers over the bulge in his leather pants, to feel his sex growing hotter, harder under her touch.

"Come here," Blake said, his voice husky. "I want you to do something for me before we start."

Erin circled to his side of the bench, turning her back on the lounge, which helped her concentrate on Blake and only Blake. From this position, she could be any blond woman; Scott would never guess her identity simply from seeing her from behind. She hadn't been to a club in years, since before she was pregnant with Abby, and he certainly wouldn't be expecting her at a VIP event.

"Kneel," Blake said, inclining his head.

She obeyed, a thrill of desire sweeping over her skin as her knees hit the floor in front of Blake. It had been so long since she'd knelt in front of a man and meant the act of submission with every bone in her body. Scott had demanded she meet him at the door every day on her knees when he got home from work, but her heart hadn't been in it, especially not the last couple of years.

But with Blake, it was like her entire being lit up from the inside. Blinding need, hot and thick, consumed her in a suffocating rush.

Her skin suddenly felt too small and the aching inside of her too big. Her pussy clamped down around its own emptiness, her nipples puckered so tightly they began to sting, and suddenly her mind flooded with images of what it would be like to meet *this* man at the door every night.

Just imagining it made her breathless.

"Do you like kneeling for me?" he asked, the tone of his voice making it clear he already knew the answer.

"Yes, sir," she said, marveling at how right it felt to call him "sir."

It was amazing how easily they transitioned from the easy banter of old friends to the world of the Dom and his obedient sub. It made her long even more fiercely for the chance to find out if their relationship could have lasted for the long haul.

"Does it make your pussy wet?" he asked, bringing her mind back to more pleasurable things. She didn't want to think about their inevitable separation.

From now on, she was focusing on enjoying the present.

She sucked in a deep breath and let it out, allowing her mind to clear as she did so. "Yes, sir."

"Show me," he said, in a whisper so soft only she could hear. "Touch yourself."

Hand trembling with excitement, Erin slid her fingers down the front of her shorts, inside her panties. She had only the tiniest tuft of hair left on her mound after shaving in the shower, but the feel of that coarse fuzz against her fingers was unbearably arousing. Touching those neatly trimmed hairs meant she was only a few centimeters away from where she was already dripping with need for Blake.

She moaned as her fingertips eased past her clit, throwing her head back, feeling her hair brush her neck as she tipped her face toward the ceiling. Now Blake would be able to see what it did to her, see how hot it made her to touch herself while he watched.

Erin dipped first one finger and then two into the cream between her legs, slowly fucking herself with her hand, amazed at how close she was to orgasm. She couldn't remember ever feeling so aroused, even during the time she'd spent with Blake in his cabin. She was hyperaware of every inch of her sensitive flesh, of Blake standing over her, of the couple a few feet away and the eager noises the female sub made as her partner tied her to the St Andrew's cross on the wall.

"Open your eyes."

She did, meeting Blake's with another moan. Just looking at him was nearly enough to make her come, right then. The heat in his gaze sent a shock of electricity zinging into nerve endings she hadn't even known she possessed. Her hand moved faster of its own accord, coaxing more heat from her body until her fingers were coated with her own arousal and her muscles trembled from being so near the edge of release.

But she knew Blake wouldn't let her tumble

over. He was too good at this to let her find release so quickly.

"Stop," he said in a ragged voice. "Show me your hand."

Without a beat of hesitation, she pulled her fingers from her pussy and held them up in the air in front of her. Blake gripped her wrist, steadying her, then leaned down and sucked both fingers into his mouth, moaning in approval.

Erin watched him clean every inch of her damp flesh, captivated by the profound pleasure so evident on his face. The man genuinely loved the flavor of her body. It wasn't a declaration of love, but it still made her throat tight with emotion to watch him taste her so thoroughly before he pulled her fingers from his mouth.

Blake made every part of her feel beautiful, desired—inside and out. When he looked at her with such obvious adoration, she felt like she could do anything, *would* do anything he asked to make sure the light in his eyes never faded. It might have been frightening if they were planning a future together—knowing she was so eager to obey Blake's every command.

But they only had tonight, and all she felt was ready.

So, so ready.

"Now you're ready." Blake echoed her thoughts. "Get up on the bench, hands down at the end with the cuffs."

CHAPTER ELEVEN

Erin

Adrenaline dumped into Erin's system as she climbed up on the bench, straddling the padded middle and positioning her knees on either side.

The second her ass was in the air and her wrists positioned down where Blake waited with the gold handcuffs, her mind began to soften, her awareness narrowing to the man cuffing her in place.

The familiar buzz of excitement and relaxation, anticipation and contentment, pulsed through her veins, making her feel more intoxicated than an entire bottle of the brandy they'd sipped at the bar could have ever accomplished. By the time Blake finished with her hands and smoothed one large, warm hand down her back, all the way to her rump, she was beyond rational thought, nothing but a bundle of nerves ready to respond.

"You may speak when asked a direct question," Blake said as he arranged her clothing with slow, deliberate movements.

First he tugged both sides of the loose-fitting satin shorts up, exposing the cheeks of her ass to the cool air, making the fabric between her legs pull tight against her clit. It was just enough stimulation to make her gasp and tremble, wishing it were Blake's fingers rubbing against her instead.

"Do you like having your ass bared for me?"

"Yes, sir." Erin sighed in pure pleasure. "So much."

"What about your tits? Would you like me to see them? To touch them?"

"Yes, sir," she said, the words turning to a moan as Blake's hands moved to her chemise, pulling at the neckline until her breasts sprung free. Her hypersensitive nipples brushing against the fabric was enough to send a fresh bolt of desire surging between her legs.

"I love these tits. I love how your nipples feel in my mouth." He captured one nipple in his hand as he spoke, plucking and tugging until Erin's breath came in little pants and needy sounds issued from the back of her throat. "I love to suck them while you ride my cock. Do you like that?"

Blake transferred his attentions to her other breast, pinching and rolling.

Frissons of excitement shot between her legs, making her voice shake when she finally managed to speak. "Yes, sir. I want you inside of me. Please."

"I'm not going to change my mind, Erin. We agreed on the terms of engagement before we left the hotel," he said, both hands busy with her nipples, making her head spin and things low in her body twist and ache.

"Please, Blake," she begged, certain she would lose her mind if she didn't feel him filling every inch of the horrible emptiness between her legs. "Please, fuck me. Please, I—"

"No. And you should know better than to ask." His fingers abandoned her breasts, making her moan with a mixture of disappointment and relief. She couldn't have taken much more without losing her mind from want, but she still felt the absence of his touch like a physical blow. "I'm disappointed."

"I wasn't asking, I was begging," Erin said, doing her best to explain herself. "Blake, please, I—"

"You were only supposed to speak when answering a direct question." Blake tucked her breasts back into her shirt. Seconds later he was circling around behind her, headed toward the selection of paddles and whips on the wall. "So I can only assume you want to be punished."

Excitement rushed across her skin, sharp and electric.

God. Yes. This was so perfect. This was exactly how she'd always dreamed a scene could be, each moment flowing into the next almost like they were working from a script.

She should have known Blake wasn't the kind to go straight to the paddle without any buildup. He needed a reason to spank her and he knew she needed it, too. He dominated the way he made love, with just the perfect amount of foreplay and a commitment to the business at hand that made her skin feel like it was going to melt clean off her bones.

"Tilt your hips, show me my ass," he commanded.

Erin obeyed, arching her back, revealing as much of her bottom as she could while still wearing her shorts.

"Beautiful," he said reverently. "You have a gorgeous ass."

His hand descended a second later, smacking her bare bottom with enough force to make Erin gasp and her body come alive. Just the sound of skin making sharp contact with skin was an aphrodisiac.

"I was going to use one of the paddles, but I think my hand is better, don't you think?" he asked, punctuating his words with stinging slaps to both mounds of her ass. The pain accentuated her pleasure, intensifying the drunken feeling spinning through her head.

"Yes. Sir." Erin's eyes slid closed and a shudder of bliss shook her body. "More, sir."

"Don't speak unless answering a question, sweetness." He intensified his efforts, his hand falling faster, harder, making her cry out and a wild laugh escape her lips. She was so wet and getting wetter by the second.

She couldn't remember ever feeling so high after only a few minutes in restraints. It made her wonder what undiscovered territory she and Blake might find if they had hours to play, if they worked their way through the rooms of equipment, until they were both so unbearably aroused Blake couldn't resist fucking her against the wall.

"This is making you wet, beautiful. Isn't it?" Blake asked, his voice caressing her sensitized flesh.

"Why don't you see for yourself, sir?"

"You want my fingers in your pussy?" He slapped her again, and again, until her already reddened ass burned.

But it was a sweet heat, driving her excitement to a place where pain and pleasure fused into one all-consuming need. The need to feel *him* touching her, owning her, punishing her, and blessing her all at the same time, until her entire body trembled with excitement.

"Yes, sir. Yes, please!" Her words ended in a cry as Blake tugged aside the scrap of fabric covering her sex and shoved his fingers inside her.

He set a punishing rhythm, driving in and out with first two fingers and then three, never ceasing his work on her stinging cheeks. Low, almost guttural sounds filled the air, but it took several seconds for Erin to realize they were coming from her own mouth. And even when she did, she couldn't bring herself to care. Blake brought out the animal in her, the sexual creature who knew no shame when she was so close to satisfaction.

"Come for me, beautiful," he commanded. "Come on my fingers. I want to feel my pussy tight on my hand."

"Blake!" She cried his name as she came and light and color flashed behind her tightly closed eyes.

The orgasm hit hard and fast, tightening her womb until it felt as if the bliss might break her. Her entire body felt like it was coming, every inch of her skin on fire, every nerve ending sending messages of ecstasy rocketing up her spinal cord, overloading her brain, making her scream.

She felt as if she'd been plunged into freezing water, the shock of the moment was so intense.

"Yes, God, yes." Blake's soft words of approval were the first thing she heard as the ringing in her ears subsided.

It felt as if she'd been in the grips of the fierce pleasure he'd given her for hours. She'd lost time somewhere between when he'd told her to come and the moment she drifted down to earth, coming to her senses enough to realize his fingers still played in and out of her slickness. It was a pleasure blackout, induced solely from the skill of the man who worked her body and mind, no controlled substances required.

She'd heard about this kind of thing, but never experienced the phenomenon, never known how elated and terrified it could make you feel.

She'd truly been out of her mind, totally dependent on her Dom to care for her while she explored the boundaries of how much pleasure one body could take. But no matter how scary it was to be so vulnerable, especially in a public place, Erin knew she was going to crave the experience again.

And again.

She was hooked with one go, like a heroin addict in the making.

Blake pulled his fingers from between her legs and repositioned her shorts before leaning down to whisper into her hair. "Was that as good as it looked, gorgeous?"

"Better," she said, shivering as he dropped kisses along her bare shoulder.

A simple kiss shouldn't be able to make her entire body begin to ache once more. But it did.

He did.

"I love you, Blake."

One large hand smoothed her hair from her face with a tenderness that threatened to break her. "I love you, too, Erin. And I always will."

And then he kissed her, softly, gently, making love to her lips with his. In every caress, in the languid way his tongue stroked into her mouth, she felt the truth of his words. He loved her, in the same soul-shattering way she loved him. It was going to cut him apart to leave her, but he was still going to do it.

He was still going to leave. That truth was in his kiss, as well.

"I think it's just about show time," he murmured against her lips, as he typed a combination of numbers into the remote control masquerading as his watch. "Are you ready?"

It took a few seconds for Erin to remember what Blake was talking about. She'd been so lost in the pleasure he'd given her, she'd forgotten all about Scott. Now she remembered, but for some reason, she felt stronger after submitting to Blake.

She was ready to face the man who had been the monster in her bed and put that dark chapter of her life behind her once and for all.

"I'm ready," Erin said. "Let's get these cuffs off."

"Yes, ma'am." He squeezed her hip, a comforting gesture that sent another surge of confidence sweeping over her. That subtle touch reminded her she wasn't alone. She had backup, at least for tonight, and she was ready to face her demons.

Good thing, because Blake had just started to work on freeing her hands when a familiar voice sounded from her left.

"Well, Erin," Scott sneered. "What a good little slut you've become. For someone else."

CHAPTER TWELVE

Erin

The way Scott said "slut" made the word sound exactly like what it was—an insult, a term used to demean a woman and make her feel small and dirty. But she wasn't small or dirty. She was loved and safe.

Blake was here, right next to her. She wasn't alone.

She drew strength from that knowledge as

she met Scott's eyes. They were nearly the same brown as Blake's, but devoid of the warmth that made Blake's so compelling. The fact that they were bloodshot didn't help. He must have been drinking before he arrived at the club.

"Scott, how are you?" Erin asked as Blake finished loosening the cuffs from around her wrists.

She climbed off the spanking bench with as much dignity as she could muster. At least all of her key areas were covered so she didn't have to suffer the embarrassment of adjusting her clothes in front of her soon-to-be ex and his new friend.

The bleached blonde with the enormous breasts was glaring at her from slightly behind Scott, but she was staying out of the way. Erin didn't anticipate encountering any resistance from her when she asked Scott to step outside for a talk. And assuming the cameras and mic were operational, she could make the suggestion at any time.

She'd seen Blake do something to his watch, but were they really online? She wished she'd been able to get confirmation from the guys in the van outside before she launched into this stage of the plan, but now there wasn't time. Scott had made the first move.

"Very well. Business is excellent, and Abby is getting so big." Scott smiled, a nasty twist of his lips that made it clear he knew how it hurt her to hear Abby's name. "She and Jill have really hit it off." He turned to the woman behind him. "Jill, this is Erin, the biological mother."

Erin bit her lip, fighting the urge to fly at Scott and tear at his face with her fingernails. *Biological* mother indeed. She was Abby's *only* mother, and there was no way in hell she was going to let another woman take her place.

"Nice to meet you," Jill said, her voice an octave higher than Erin had expected it to be. She sounded like a little girl, something Erin was sure Scott enjoyed.

He loved feeling like a big man, and he

needed all the help he could get from the sub in his life to get the job done. Scott only felt Dominant when everyone else around him was performing at less than their potential. He'd never had what it took to master a woman who was more than a two-dimensional Barbie doll. He wasn't strong enough.

The realization made Erin feel taller, stronger, and certain for the first time that she was going to win this battle. Her daughter would be in her arms by the end of the night and Scott would be on his way to a restraining order and maybe some time in a jail cell with men who would show him what it felt like to be an abused partner.

"I wish I could say the same, Jill. But it's not nice to meet you," Erin said, maintaining the pleasant smile on her face even when Scott's expression went from smug to dangerous. "I'm not in a nice mood. Scott has been keeping me from my daughter and it's time that ended. Don't you agree, Scott?"

"I think you should watch your mouth," Scott snapped. "And remember what we decided about this."

"No one tells Erin to watch her mouth. Except me." Blake stepped closer, until he loomed over the much shorter Scott. "You're not in charge here anymore."

"Erin, outside. Now. We need to talk. In private." Scott barked orders with as much authority as ever, but Erin saw the spark of fear in his eyes. He saw there was a bigger dog in town, hence the sudden urge to get her alone. "Obviously your memory needs a little refreshing."

He was playing right into their hands. Erin's pulse raced faster as she silently prayed everything was going to work out the way they'd hoped.

"May I go, Master?" Erin turned back to Blake, lingering on the last word. Scott had always wanted her to call him "Master," but she'd refused.

She was a submissive, and she loved to be

mastered, but for some reason, the term never tasted right in her mouth. "Sir," she liked just fine, but "Master" made her feel like one of those male slaves who went around licking their mistress's boots.

Or the hunchback guy that worked with Frankenstein, which wasn't a visual she enjoyed during sex.

"She can go." Blake put a hand at the small of her back as she turned to face Scott. "But if you hurt her, I'll make you bleed."

Jill's eyes widened into big blue saucers, but there was arousal in their depths, mixing with her fear. Erin couldn't blame the other woman. Blake was irresistible, especially compared to a worm like Scott.

"Touch me and I'll have you thrown out of here so fast your head will swim, he-man," Scott said, his voice shaking.

Erin stifled the strange urge to giggle. *He-man?* That was the best insult he could come up with on the spur of the moment? This was the Dom she'd lived in fear of for years? He was nothing but a sad, insecure little man. She'd been a fool to fear him, but that was ending right now.

It was payback time.

"Make your threats," Blake said, his tone still calm and even. "But make sure you listen to what Erin has to say and know that I back her up completely. You can't get away with bullying her anymore."

Truer words had never been spoken. Even without Blake there beside her, Erin knew what he'd said would be true. She was different, tougher, and as ready as she'd ever be to finish this thing with Scott.

"Come with me, Erin. Jill, wait at the bar." Scott turned and headed for the front door.

Erin took one last look back at Blake, drawing strength from the confident expression on his face, and followed.

CHAPTER THIRTEEN

Erin

Erin's heart raced as she tailed Scott back through the crowded lounge area. The bar and surrounding tables were packed and the alcohol flowing freely. It was only a matter of time before everyone would be loosened up enough to start heading back into the playrooms.

She knew how it worked. She used to be

one of those people who needed a few glasses of wine to be in the mood to start a scene, but not anymore.

Now, a look from Blake and a few well-chosen words were enough to banish all of her inhibitions.

"I'll be coming back in," Scott said to the bouncer at the exit before shoving past, not bothering to hold the door for her.

But then, manners had never been his strong suit, and he wasn't exactly a happy camper right now. She took a deep breath, hoping that unhappiness would work in her favor.

"I'll be coming back in, too." Erin smiled at the large man working the door, and obediently held out her hand to get it stamped for readmission.

"The door closes in thirty minutes, so be sure you're back before then," the bouncer said kindly before turning his attention back to the lobby.

Erin nodded and pushed through the door,

apprehension skittering across her skin. The nearby street lamps illuminated the sidewalk, but it was pretty deserted outside the club. Everyone was still going in, not coming out.

Don't worry. The boys in the van are watching. You're safe.

But the thought didn't give her much comfort when Scott ducked into the shadowed alley beside the club and spun to face her, fury distorting his features.

It was darker here than out on the sidewalk, but she could still see him clearly, still see the way he had been transformed by rage. It made her mouth run dry with fear, even though she knew she shouldn't be surprised by the strength of his response.

She'd *never* defied him. She'd talked back and gone against his wishes when it came to Dom-sub stuff, sure, but she'd never said a contrary word when it came to big decisions. Scott had always been the walking boss in their relationship, and he obviously didn't take well to having his authority questioned.

"What exactly do you think you're trying to pull, Erin?" he asked, the vein on his forehead pulsing unhealthily.

"I'm not trying to pull anything," she said, hating the way her voice trembled. "I just want to see my daughter. I deserve to be a part of her life."

"You don't deserve shit." He stepped closer, and she had to fight the urge to back away. She couldn't give him an inch or he'd take a mile. She knew that, but it was still hard to stand her ground with her knees beginning to quake. "You violated our contract the day you walked out. I don't owe you a dime."

"I'm not asking for money. I just want to be Abby's mother."

"You think you're fit to be Abby's mother? A slut like you, out getting her ass spanked at some club by a stranger?" Scott moved nearer still, until she could smell the alcohol on his breath. "I saw you on the bench. You were grunting like a pig when you came. It made me sick to think my daughter came from that diseased hole between your legs."

"I am not diseased," Erin ground out, but the insult still hurt. "And if going to clubs is a problem, I'll stop. Though I have to say, it seems pretty hypocritical that you get to do whatever you want while I—"

Her words ended in a shocked gasp as Scott's hand snapped out, catching her across the face.

He'd hit her.

He'd finally done it and as her hand came to cup her stinging skin she realized she'd known he would. Eventually. When his words stopped getting the job done. Her right cheek burned and her ears rang from the impact, but she still refused to back away.

Instead, she stood up even straighter, glaring up at Scott, hoping the camera was catching every second of his abuse. "You can't bully me anymore. And any man who would hit the mother of his child isn't fit to be a father."

"Watch your mouth, bitch," he panted, his

breath coming as fast as if he'd just stepped off the track. He was weirdly out of breath for a man who worked out three times a week. But maybe he'd given up the runs along the beach. He certainly looked thinner than he had just a few weeks ago. "I don't take orders from whores."

"I'm not a whore. I never touched another man while we were together. I was faithful," she said in a calm, even tone. "I know you can't say the same. So in my book that makes *you* the whore."

Erin was prepared for the blow this time, but that didn't make it hurt any less. Stars danced behind her eyes and her cheekbone throbbed and she had a feeling that strike was going to leave a bruise.

Good, more evidence against the bastard.

The thought made her smile. "Do you hit Abby, too, Scott?" she asked. "Is that the kind of father you are?"

"I treat Abby like a princess," he snapped.

"Keeping her away from her mother isn't

treating her like a princess," Erin said, mind racing, trying to figure out what to say next.

She had to get tape of Scott threatening Abby, not just slapping his ex-wife around. She needed to prove to the court that Scott was a danger to his daughter if she wanted a shot at getting sole custody.

"She needs me in her life," she continued. "I was home with her every day since she was born. She must miss me. It must scare and upset her to—"

"I'm going to say this one more time— Abby is better off without you. Stay away from her, or you're going to be very sorry. I can promise you that."

Oh, God. This was it. This was *it.*

"Nothing could make me more sorry than being kept from Abby another day," she said, the tears in her voice as real as the words she spoke. It had only been three weeks since she'd seen Abby, but it felt like a lifetime. "She needs me, and I need to be a part of my daughter's life."

"Your daughter won't have a life if you keep this up, Erin." He smiled, a cold sneer that made her heart ache. This was the bastard she'd chosen as the father of her child. Abby deserved so much better. "I wasn't making idle threats when I said I'd kill her before I'd let her be raised by a slut like you."

"Scott, listen to yourself," she said, heart pounding in her chest. The words still scared her to death, even knowing there was a plan in place to get Abby out of Scott's house and keep her safe. "That's our baby you're talking about, an innocent child. How can you even—"

"If you don't sign the divorce decree in the next week, or if I find out you've hired a lawyer, Abby will have a horrible accident." He paused, eyes drifting to a place above her head.

He sniffed and swiped the back of his hand across his nose. "I was thinking the pool out back. She's crawling so fast now. If the nanny were to leave the door open and turn her back for a few minutes...well, it doesn't take that long for a child to drown."

Erin's throat grew tight and tears stung at the back of her eyes, but she didn't cry. What Scott said wasn't going to happen, she wasn't going to *let* it happen. "You're a monster."

"Maybe." He shrugged, and his smile returned as his eyes met hers once more. "But I'd rather Abby be raised by a monster than a penniless whore. At least she'll have a chance at a future, to grow up to be something more than a tramp who takes her clothes off for money."

Erin swallowed the retort on the tip of her tongue. He didn't care to make the distinction between a model and a stripper or he would have done so. Arguing with Scott was a waste of time. Besides, she had what she needed. Scott's threats were captured on tape. If all was going according to plan, Rafe was already on his way to the house to get Abby.

She could walk away right now and never say a word to this creep again.

Instead, she stood her ground. Until this moment, she hadn't realized how much unfinished business there was between the two of them. But now, all the questions she hadn't dared to ask in the last two pain-filled years flooded to the surface.

"Why do you hate me so much?" she asked softly, genuinely curious.

His bloodshot eyes widened before narrowing once more. "I don't hate you. I feel nothing for you except disgust."

"Then why didn't you ask for a divorce sooner?" she asked. "Obviously our marriage wasn't what either of us—"

"Our marriage was fine," Scott said, the emotion in his voice surprising her. "Everything was fine until you up and left with our daughter."

"Scott, our marriage was not fine," Erin said, baffled that even he could be that deluded. "Nothing I did seemed to please you. Not since I got pregnant with Abby."

He shook his head. "That's not true."

"You didn't even want to touch me," she said. "We hadn't had sex in almost two years by the time I left. How can you call that fine?"

"So you wanted to get fucked? Is that it?" he asked, taking an aggressive step forward. "I'll fuck you right now if that's what you want."

"No, it isn't." This time, she took a step back. A slap or two she could handle, but if Scott tried to touch her intimately she'd take Blake up on the offer to make him bleed. "But when I was pregnant with Abby, and just after, I wanted to be close to you. And sex is a part of that. It's part of a good marriage, surely you can't disagree."

Scott's eyes dropped to the pavement between them, and he ran a frustrated hand through his hair. For the first time, Erin noticed that it was thinning on top. Scott was twelve years older than she was, but she'd never really thought about the age difference until now, when he suddenly looked far older than his thirty-six years.

"I just..." His voice trailed off, but Erin didn't push. Pushing Scott only made him angry.

He took a deep breath and let it out slowly. Several uncomfortable seconds passed before he finally spoke again. "By the time Abby was born, it seemed like we'd lost our place. You were so focused on the baby. I felt like you didn't need me anymore. It hurt."

Of all the things she'd thought she'd hear tonight, Scott opening up about his feelings was the very last. She was stunned.

"I needed you more than ever," Erin said, then pushed on, refusing to let Scott play the victim. "But it seemed like you hated me. I mean, talk about hurt. Every time you told me how unattractive you found me, it felt like I was being cut open. It hurt. So much."

He finally lifted his head, facing her with uncertain eyes. "What if I said I didn't mean it? That I'd made a mistake?"

"What?" She could safely say she'd never been more confused. What the hell was he saying?

"What if I said I didn't mean all those things I said, or the stuff about Abby?" He paused, licking his lips, the words obviously far from easy to speak. "Would you think about coming back?"

"You want me back." Erin didn't know whether to laugh or cry or both. "But you're the one who filed for divorce."

"That's only because you left me. How could you just *leave* like that, Erin?" he asked, anguish clear in his voice. "I came home from work and you were just gone. I thought someone had kidnapped you. I was scared out of my mind."

"I was scared, too," she said. "I was afraid you'd do something to me or Abby if I told you I was leaving."

"You should have known I'd never hurt you. Never," he said, the passion in his eyes making it clear he believed every word. He reached for her, but she stepped away again, shaking her head in disbelief.

"Scott, you hurt me with your words for years," Erin said. "You tore me down until there was nothing left of my self-esteem. And you just hit me—twice."

He scowled. "I was angry. And I have every right to be. You don't know what it did to me, seeing another man's fingers inside *my* wife. It made me crazy."

"Crazy enough to threaten to kill our daughter? Was that something you didn't mean, too?" Erin held her breath, wondering if the men in the van were still recording, and how all the strange, unexpected turns in this conversation would impact their case against Scott.

If he confessed to lying about intending to kill Abby, would that make a difference to the judge who reviewed their case?

Had she endangered her future with her daughter because she didn't know when to keep her big mouth shut?

"Come back to me," Scott said softly. "Come home with me right now, and you'll never have to find out."

Erin shook her head. "I can't."

"Yes, you can. Ditch that caveman and come home. We'll send the housekeeper over to your apartment to get your things tomorrow." He paused and a smile stretched across his face, reminding her of the man he'd been when they were first married. The man she'd thought she loved, until she'd reunited with Blake and remembered what real love felt like. "You could be holding Abby in half an hour. You can even bring her into the bed to sleep with us if you want, the way you wanted to do when she was teething."

"No," Erin said, hoping he heard the finality in the word. "I'm never coming back to you. I don't love you anymore. I'm not sure I ever did."

His smile faded, and the terrifying Scott returned. "Is it that man you're with? Are you *in love* with him now?"

"Yes, I am. I love him with all my heart," she said, the words out of her mouth before she could think better of them.

It only took a few seconds for her to realize the error of her decision, but by then it was too late.

Scott's hands were already latched around her throat.

CHAPTER FOURTEEN

Blake

Blake was through the door the second Steve texted, saying Erin needed backup, cursing himself for letting her stay outside so long.

He'd gotten the first call from the van five minutes ago. Everything had gone according to plan and Rafe was already on his way to get Abby. There was no reason to leave Erin alone with that waste of human flesh a second longer.

But he'd wanted to let her handle the situation, to show her he believed she was strong enough to manage Scott alone. After all, he was going to Miami in a few days. He wouldn't be here to help her anymore. She'd have to stand on her own two feet.

But she'll have a restraining order by then, jackass.

He *was* a jackass, and now Erin was going to have the bruises to prove it.

Blake charged around the corner and into the alley beside the club, where Scott had Erin backed against the brick wall with his hands at her throat.

Immediately, his blood ran hot and his vision filled with red.

He'd warned the bastard he'd make him bleed if he hurt Erin. Now he was going to prove he was a man of his word.

"Blake, wait!" Erin shouted as she shoved her ex-husband's hands from her throat. Scott slumped forward, collapsing against her.

"I think he's passed out or—" Erin's words

ended in a surprised yip as Scott suddenly began to shake, his body jerking like he'd stuck his hand in a light socket.

A moment later the other man fell to the ground, convulsing as his eyes rolled back in his head.

"What's happening?" Erin flattened herself against the wall, staring with wide eyes at the man writhing at her feet.

Blake reached over the twitching body and grabbed Erin under the arms, lifting her over her ex before setting her gently down on the concrete on the other side. "Go, tell the woman at the desk to call 911."

She nodded and raced toward the door, but not before Blake saw the red swelling on her left cheek. The bastard had hit her. She'd have a bruise tomorrow at the very least, if not a full-on black eye. The knowledge would have been enough to make him knock Scott out— if the cowardly fuck hadn't been out cold already.

"Piece of shit," Blake muttered as he knelt

by the other man, who was finally lying still.

A check of his pulse revealed he was still alive—unfortunately—though his heart was racing like he'd run a marathon, not spent a few minutes slapping around his wife. The speeding pulse didn't seem natural for a young man who looked to be in good shape. Neither did the cold, clammy skin.

Blake's suspicions were confirmed when he pried open Scott's eyes and found them bloodshot and his pupils widely dilated. He'd been on something, probably cocaine if Blake had to guess. That would explain the racing heart and his out-of-control temper.

"What happened? Is he dead?" A man in a suit whom Blake had seen roaming the club earlier rushed out the door with Erin close behind. "I'm Jace the owner."

"I told him we were having an argument and he started shaking and collapsed," Erin said, staying back a few paces as Jace came to stand just behind Blake.

"I think he had a seizure, or maybe a

stroke," Blake said. "Probably drug-induced. I'm a tattoo artist. By law, we're not supposed to work on anyone who's been using, so I've learned to read the signs." Blake stood. "He's still breathing and his pulse is accelerated, but steady. I don't think there's much we can do for him until the paramedics arrive."

"Drugs?" Erin asked. "Scott's been using drugs?"

"Son of a bitch." Jace sighed and shook his head. "I thought he looked bad tonight, but I didn't want to say anything. He usually keeps it respectable, and he's never brought anything into the club."

Blake nodded. "So you think he's been using for a while?"

"I've only known him a few months," Jace said with a shrug. "But yeah, he seems to have a pretty decent coke habit."

"A habit." Erin cursed, glaring at the man at her feet as if she'd like to kick his prone body. "While he was supposed to be taking care of an eleven-month-old. I'm going to kill him."

"You may not have to," the club owner said as sirens sounded in the distance. "I had a friend of mine, old college football buddy, died of combination stroke and heart attack from a coke overdose a few years back."

"Oh, my God," Erin said, her voice soft as her hand flew to her mouth.

Blake wrapped his arms around her, pulling her close as an ambulance pulled into the parking lot. "He'll be fine. He's going to live to regret ever laying a hand on you in anger."

"You saw?" Erin asked, the face she tilted up to his washed red from the flashing lights.

"I saw this." He brushed his knuckles softly over her cheek, feeling his guts twist when she winced. "It made me want to kill him myself."

"It doesn't hurt that bad. I'll be fine." She lowered her voice even though Jace had already left to meet the EMTs as they jumped from the ambulance. "Is Rafe on his way to get Abby?"

"He left ten minutes ago. I should be

getting a call soon. You'd better tell the paramedics what happened." Blake urged her to go and watched Erin fill in the paramedics, his mind racing.

Scott's unexpected collapse could either work for them or against them. If the nanny reported the baby missing the night after her employer overdosed at the same party his wife had been attending, there was a chance the police might come around, asking Erin questions. But if Rafe hadn't taken Abby yet, there might still be a way for this to end even better than they'd hoped.

His cell was out of his pocket a second later. Thankfully, Rafe answered on the second ring. "Hey, do you have Abby yet?"

"Not yet," he whispered, "but I'm on the property, so can this conversation wait?"

"No, it can't. Get out and go wait in your car," Blake said. "I'll give you a call in a few minutes. We've had an unexpected development."

Rafe sighed. "All right, boss. You're

running this show."

Blake snapped the phone shut and then open again. He waited until Scott was loaded into the ambulance and the owner vanished back into the club before he put the phone in Erin's hand. "Here, call the nanny. Tell her what happened and that you're on your way to pick up Abby."

Erin blinked. "Rafe doesn't have her yet?"

"I called him and told him the plan had changed," Blake said with a reassuring smile. "This will work out much better."

"Right, of course." Erin shook her head as if to clear it. "I didn't even think, but this will make my case, won't it? Even without the threats, a judge isn't going to give custody to a man with a documented drug habit."

"And I'd say a hospitalization for overdose is pretty good documentation."

Erin smiled, a weary stretch of her lips. "I wouldn't have wished this on Scott, but it feels so good to know I'm not going to lose Abby again. God, when I think of what could have happened to her…"

She sucked in a shaky breath. "What if she'd found drugs in the house? She sticks everything in her mouth, and it wouldn't take much cocaine to *kill* a twenty-four-pound baby."

"Don't think about it. Just make that call then we'll get on the road." Blake squeezed her hand. "You'll be holding Abby in thirty minutes or less."

This time, Erin's smile was bright enough to light the entire street. It made Blake wish he was going to be around to watch her learn how to smile and relax again. He was going to miss Erin, more than he'd thought possible, but his leaving was for the best. The events of tonight had only proven how dangerous a failed Dom-sub relationship could become.

Erin would be safer without a controlling man in her life. And he was going to do his best to convince her of that on their way to pick up her daughter. If there was ever a time for Erin to come back to the kink-free side of the fence, this was it.

Blake wished the thought didn't make him sad, but it did. Which just went to show how bad he would be for her.

"Okay, we're good to go. She said she'd have Abby's things packed by the time we get there." Erin squealed and threw her arms around his neck. "She's coming home with us, Blake. Right now!"

"Speaking of the hotel," Blake said, hugging Erin for the briefest second before pulling away, "why don't we run by and grab some more appropriate clothes on the way? It would be better if we didn't show up to meet the nanny in club gear."

"Right, of course." There was a hurt look in her eyes as she turned toward his car, but Blake did his best to ignore it. They both knew this had to end, no sense in pretending otherwise.

Tomorrow, he'd help Erin and Abby get settled in Erin's apartment and start the necessary legal paperwork. The day after tomorrow he'd be on a plane on his way to Miami. Once he was there, he'd throw himself into getting the new parlor ready to open and forgetting he'd ever seen Erin again, let alone lost his heart to her a second time.

It wasn't going to be easy, but he was used to living with a gaping hole in his chest. He'd been doing it for years, ever since sixteen-year-old Erin had left Carson City.

Blake popped the locks on the Expedition and climbed behind the wheel, his thoughts leaving a sour taste in his mouth.

"What's wrong?" she asked, meeting his eyes with a troubled look.

"Nothing." He forced a smile and started the car. There was no sense dwelling on the past. Their past didn't matter.

It was time to grow up and move on, and finally put all those old dreams behind him.

LILI VALENTE

CHAPTER FIFTEEN

Two months later

Erin

The doorbell rang, shocking Erin out of a sound sleep. A quick glance at the clock revealed it was barely six in the morning.

Who in their right mind would be stopping by for a visit at this hour?

Maybe it's not someone in their right mind. Maybe it's him, maybe he was finally released from the hospital and he's not in the mood to obey the restraining order.

Erin vaulted into a seated position. She hadn't called to check on Scott's status in a few days, but surely he couldn't be ready to go home yet. His stroke had been massive and the doctors said he'd need months of physical therapy before he was anywhere close to fully functional again. They'd also promised to call her before they released him, since they knew about his history and the restraining order in place keeping him from seeing his ex-wife or child.

The bell rang again, making her heart leap into her throat. "Just a second," she called out, jumping out of bed and taking a quick peek in Abby's crib.

The baby was still asleep, thank God. Nothing could wake her until she was ready to get up, so hopefully she'd snooze straight through whatever madness might ensue if it really was Scott at the door.

One thing was for certain, no one was

going to take Abby from her again. She was going to make damn sure of that.

She had the gun out of its shoe box on the top shelf of her closet and in her hand in seconds. If Scott violated the restraining order and tried to hurt her or Abby again, she'd shoot him and deal with the fallout later. Even standing trial for murder in self-defense would be better than letting him take Abby away.

The past two months alone with Abby had made her love for her daughter even fiercer than it had been before. She'd do anything it took to keep her safe.

"Who is it?" Erin asked once she was at the door, buying herself time as she peered through the peephole and saw the last person she'd expected.

"It's Rafe," he said, the words barely out of his mouth before she threw open the door. He took in her rumpled hair and pj's with an apologetic smile. "Sorry about the early hour."

"It's okay. Come in," Erin said, opening

the door wider, scanning the stairs behind him, a foolish part of her hoping she'd see Blake.

But she should know better. Blake hadn't even called to say hi since he'd left for Miami. He didn't want anything more to do with her. He'd made that abundantly clear.

"I'm on my way to Hawaii and only have a six-hour layover," Rafe said as he waltzed past her into the apartment. "Nice gun. You bring that to the door to greet all your visitors?"

"Only the ones who show up unexpectedly who I think might be my ex-husband."

Rafe arched a brow. "That's pretty tough. I'm impressed."

"You do what you gotta do." Erin turned back to the closet to put the gun back in its hiding place. That was the good thing about a studio apartment—everything was in easy reach. "Can I get you some coffee or something?"

"No, like I said, I've got to run in a few." Rafe paused, running a distracted hand through his thick hair. "I just needed to talk to you. In person."

"What about?" Erin asked, already imagining the worst. "Is Blake okay? He's not hurt or sick, is he? I mean, he'd probably have to be a lot worse than hurt for you to come all the way out here, but—"

"He is. A lot worse."

"Oh, God." Tears sprung to her eyes and she barely made it to the couch before her knees gave out. The thought of Blake suffering was too much to take standing up. "What happened?"

"You happened." Rafe took the armchair across from her, settling in like he'd visited a hundred times before. "The man's a complete wreck."

Erin didn't know whether to be relieved or pissed that Rafe had scared her half to death. "What do you mean he's a wreck?"

"He's a mess. He can't concentrate on his work, he's a cranky asshole, and he acts like Miami is the seventh level of hell, not one of the most happening cities on the planet." Rafe pulled a pack of cigarettes from his coat pocket. "I swear to God, he's lost his mind. He's even grown a beard if you can imagine. He looks like a serial killer."

"I didn't know you smoked," Erin said.

"I don't, but I'm thinking about starting." He flicked a cigarette from the pack and placed it between his lips. "Got some women trouble of my own."

Erin's brow furrowed. "Sorry to hear that, but you can't smoke in here."

"Right. Sorry. So…" He stared at her over the coffee table, an expectant look in his eye.

She shook her head. "I don't know what you want me to say."

"Say you'll take this." He reached into the inside pocket of his coat and pulled out a plane ticket, which he handed over. "And use it."

Erin picked up the ticket and glanced at the destination. "You want me to go to Kauai with you?"

"Oh, God. No." He snatched the ticket back and fished around in his other pocket. "This is your ticket. Sorry, I've been up for two days."

"Miami," Erin said, not even touching the ticket this time. Abby chose that moment to start snuffling and squirming in her crib.

Thank. God. Saved by the baby.

"Yeah, Miami. You should go. He needs you," Rafe said, his voice sincere. "Believe me, I'm not the type to say that kind of thing unless it's true. I'm worried about him."

Erin opened her mouth, then closed it, then opened it again, but still couldn't sort out what to say.

A part of her wanted to take the ticket and go to Blake, but the voice of reason wasn't buying. Blake had made it clear he didn't want a future with her, and he wasn't the one who had shown up on her doorstep. If he'd really changed his mind and was miserable without her, wouldn't he be here himself?

"Mama," Abby called in her sweet, singsong morning voice. "Mama."

Erin smiled, knowing she'd never get tired of hearing that first thing in the morning. "Hold on, give me a few minutes."

She vaulted off the couch, scooping Abby up from her crib and pressing a kiss to her warm, soft neck before laying her on the changing table. As soon as Abby had a clean diaper, Erin propped her on her hip as she crossed to the tiny kitchenette to fix Abby's bottle.

The pediatrician had suggested Erin start buying the soy formula for toddlers, but she couldn't bring herself to put Abby's milk in a sippy cup. She wasn't ready to let those baby bottle days go just yet, especially considering Abby was probably the only child she'd ever have. She didn't want to have another baby on her own and she couldn't imagine ever getting married again…unless it was to Blake.

But that was yet another reason not to go to Miami. Blake had made it clear they had no future and hadn't expressed any interest in being a father to another man's child. He'd only held Abby for a few minutes before he'd fled the hotel room like he'd seen a ghost, not held a baby.

"She's beautiful. Looks just like you," Rafe said, smiling as Erin settled back in on the couch with Abby on her lap.

"Thanks." She frowned as she handed the bottle over to Abby, who liked to hold it herself now that she was an entire year old. "But I have to tell you, Rafe, I'm surprised to see you. I didn't get the feeling you liked me much."

"I didn't," he said, tapping his pack of cigarettes on his knuckles. "I thought you were using Blake to get your kid back."

"But now you've changed your mind?"

He sighed. "I've changed my mind about a few things. Especially where the heart is concerned." He paused, meeting her eyes. "You love him."

"More than anything, except Abby," Erin said, not seeing the sense in hiding her feelings. "But that doesn't mean we have a future."

"I think it does. Blake loves you more than anything in the world. He's got it in his head he's no good for you or something, but I swear he's the best man I know. He's all heart under the big scary act."

Erin felt her throat grow tight and a bubble of hope expand in her chest, making her dizzy. "I know he is. But he told me to stay away from him. It's the last thing he said before he left."

"Listen, I know you guys have got this kinky Dominant and submissive thing going on," Rafe said, making Erin smile at the obvious discomfort in his tone. "But even the 'boss' needs to be told what's what sometimes. Blake is all mixed up. So just take that ticket and go tell him to quit being an asshole. You three belong together, I feel it in my gut."

He pulled an envelope out of his pocket and set it on the table next to the plane ticket.

"These are directions to the shop and Blake's condo. I took the liberty of having a key made to his place in case you decide to make yourself at home. He's been working the early shift at the shop, twelve to eight."

Erin bit her lip, trying to fight the excitement making her heart beat faster but finding it impossible. Rafe wasn't a hopeless romantic; he was a practical man, even a cynical one. If he was here, insisting Blake was lost without her, she had damned well better believe it.

"Let me ask you one question," she said.

Rafe nodded. "Shoot."

"Is that ticket one-way?"

He smiled. "It sure is."

She returned his grin. "Good. Because if I'm going to do this, I'm going to do it right."

"Good." The warmth in his dark eyes finally made her see why this was a man who made women swoon. Rafe was a gorgeous human being when he let his softer side show. "A woman after my own heart. Though I did get a round-trip ticket to Kauai. Two, actually. I plan on bringing someone home with me."

"The woman who inspired the change of heart?" Erin asked, happy for the man.

"Yeah. I was pretty sure I hated her until I realized I'm fucking crazy about her." He frowned as he crossed to the door. "Amazing what you learn about yourself when you hear someone's eloped with another man."

"Oh, no," Erin said. "I'm sorry."

"That's all right," Rafe said with another heartbreaker grin. "I'm going to get there before the ceremony and talk sense into her. You want me to help you pack anything before I go? The next direct flight leaves at eleven o'clock. I assume you'll want to be on that one. No sense leaving that man down there to suffer any longer."

Erin glanced around the room at the furnishings that had come with the studio and the very few things she'd managed to bring with her and Abby when they left Scott the first time. She wasn't going to be sad to leave the place that had been their home for the past two months. "No, I think I can throw our clothes in a couple of suitcases and box up the rest of the stuff before we need to catch a cab. There's not that much here."

"All right, then, I guess I'll be heading out." He paused and turned to catch her eye. "You're really going, right?"

"I am." The last of her resistance faded away as she imagined how amazing it would be to see Blake again.

"Thank you," Rafe said, vulnerability in his eyes she'd never seen before. "And don't let him tell you no."

"Thank you." She smiled. "I won't."

As she watched Rafe leave, she realized she'd never meant anything more.

CHAPTER SIXTEEN

Blake

"You want a sandwich from the Cuban bakery?" Garret, one of the Miami studio's most talented artists, stood at the door looking like the last thing he wanted to do was bring Blake a sandwich or a *pastelito de guayaba.* "They've got those hot ham and cheese ones and the pastries go half price after seven o'clock."

Garrett looked like he'd prefer to run straight into the night and keep running until he was as far away from his boss as he could possibly get. But Blake couldn't really blame the man. He hadn't been a bundle of sweetness and light the past two months.

Rabid bear with anger-management issues was a more apt description.

Blake sighed. He had to step up his people skills. Missing Erin so badly it felt like his guts had spilled out all over the floor was no excuse for alienating his entire staff.

"No, thanks. I'm getting ready to head out. I've been here since noon," Blake said, forcing a smile. "Good work today. I liked that portrait piece you started."

"Thanks." Garret's thin face lit up, making him look even younger than his twenty-one years. He was the youngest of the three new artists they'd hired for the Miami opening, but had a gift for ink not many possessed at any age. "I'm pumped to finish it. Nice change from the average job."

"Yeah. It'll be a great addition to your portfolio. Catch you tomorrow."

"Later," Garret threw over his shoulder as he darted out the door.

There. Blake had made an effort to be nice. Now he could sleep soundly tonight.

Right. He hadn't slept more than four hours straight since he left L.A. At this rate, mooning over Erin was going to make him old before his time. He already had permanent circles under his eyes, but he wasn't too worried about them. He figured they complemented his beard and fleshed out the "slightly deranged" look.

"Be sure to lock up before you go, and make Tony walk you to your car so you get there safe," Blake told Nina, the petite brunette filling in for Delilah behind the front desk while their usual office manager was on her combination wedding-honeymoon.

He never would have pegged Dee for the romantic elopement type, but she'd certainly seemed thrilled to go say "I do" to the investment banker who'd swept her off her feet. He was happy for her. It was nice to see someone having success in the relationship department.

"Sure thing, see you tomorrow," Nina said, wiggling her fingers his way.

Blake patted his pocket, making sure his keys were still there, feeling like he was forgetting something as he headed out the back door. He wondered if he'd ever get used to not carrying a coat in the winter. It was late January, but the temperature rarely dipped below the high sixties. It was one of the things Rafe loved about Miami, but Blake hadn't been able to work up the same enthusiasm for shorts and beach time year-round.

He hadn't been able to work up much enthusiasm for anything besides missing Erin, replaying every moment they'd spent together, fantasizing about the feel of her bare skin against his and the way she drove him wild with just a kiss.

"Give it a rest, man," he grumbled to

himself as he guided his car through the busy streets and then onto the quieter avenue leading down to his beachside condo.

He'd made his decision and he was going to stand by it. This was best for Erin. She didn't need another volatile man in her life putting her and her daughter in danger. He should stop torturing himself and concentrate on getting the hell over Erin and moving on.

Too bad that was easier said than done.

Maybe a stiff drink or two would help him get to sleep. He pushed open the door to his condo, debating scotch or vodka on the rocks, but froze before he took a step inside.

Someone was there. He could feel it.

"Goodness, Rafe was right." Her voice came from across the shadowed room, near the windows that overlooked the ocean, making his skin prickle. "Even in the dark, I can tell you look awful."

Blake tensed, his hand gripping the door handle, shock and excitement kicking up his heart rate. It was Erin, no doubt in his mind.

Or maybe all *in* his mind. Maybe he'd finally gone crazy enough to start hallucinating her voice. There was one way to find out.

He flicked on the lights, his chest and things lower in his body tightening as he took in the woman seated in his leather easy chair. Erin was decked out in a black corset and thigh-high stockings. Her hair tumbled around her shoulders in soft curls, and her lips shone with something pink and glossy. She was a fantasy come to life and even more beautiful than he remembered.

Too bad he had to send her on her way.

"What are you doing here?" he asked gruffly. "Are you in trouble? Is it Scott?"

"No, he's still in the hospital," she said with a smile. "Besides, I've got a restraining order and the paperwork is filed. He didn't even fight for partial custody. Now it's just a matter of waiting four more months for the divorce to be final. California has a mandatory waiting period."

"Well…good, I'm happy for you. But you need to go." Blake gritted his teeth as he gestured to the hallway. "Get dressed and get out."

"No." She stood in one smooth, easy motion and stalked across the room, her high heels accentuating her long, long legs. She didn't stop until she stood less than a foot away, close enough for him to smell the addictive scent of her perfume and the spicier smell that was all Erin. "Close the door."

"I think we've established you're not the one who gives orders, Erin."

"Close the door, Blake. I won't ask again." She pulled a mini flogger from behind her back and held it up between them.

They both knew she couldn't do him any damage with that tiny toy or anything else, but for some reason, Blake found himself letting the door swing shut. The look in her eyes was like nothing he'd ever seen. The woman was determined, and channeling some serious Dominant energy.

"Now, I'm going to talk and you're going to listen," she said, placing one hand in the center of his chest and shoving him back against the door. Even that small touch was enough to send a shock through his body, and blood surging to his cock. "First of all, you look terrible. What have you done to yourself?"

"I grew a beard," he said, surprised to hear how penitent he sounded as if he were a sub who knew he had displeased his Mistress.

"A beard that's crawling halfway down your neck. Poorly maintained facial hair is flat out gross, Blake." She narrowed her eyes, searching his face. "And you've got circles under your eyes. Are you drinking too much?"

"Nope, just not sleeping enough."

"And why aren't you sleeping enough?" she asked, a hint of softness in her eyes. She expected to hear something about how much he missed her, but he wasn't going to oblige. He had to get her to leave. Her and her daughter's safety was more important than anything they felt for each other.

"I've been busy fucking beautiful women," he said, keeping the words casual. "I'm expecting someone in an hour, so if you could get your things and be out of here by—"

"Bullshit," she said with a lazy smile. "You haven't slept with anyone since you left L.A."

He scowled. "How would you know?"

"I don't think you'd be this hard if you'd been such a busy boy." Erin slid her hand down over his engorged cock, drawing a groan from the back of his throat. She leaned closer, whispering her next words against his lips. "Poor Blake. This feels like it hurts, but I'm here to take the pain away."

"Stop," Blake said, easing her hands away. "Listen, I understand what you're trying to do, but—"

"No, you don't understand. If you understood you'd know you should quit trying to get rid of me," she said, her Dominant act faltering a bit. "Rafe told me how you've been, Blake, and I've been the same. Even with Abby back, it still feels like something's missing since you left. It's like a piece of me is gone, and I can't remember how to be happy without it."

"Erin, please. I'm not good for you and Abby. It's better this way."

Her beautiful face pulled into a frown. "Rafe said something about that, too, that you've convinced yourself you're bad news or something stupid."

"Now you're calling me stupid?" Blake laughed despite himself. "See, this wouldn't work. A big bad Dominant man doesn't put up with his sub calling him names."

Erin stepped closer, catching his eye with a look so intense he couldn't bring himself to look away. "Listen to me. You are not a big bad Dom. You are Blake, an amazing man who happens to enjoy power-exchange games in the bedroom. Being a Dom is part of what you are, but it isn't *who* you are."

"Then who am I?" he asked softly. "If you're seeing things so clearly."

"You're the man I love," she said, her eyes glistening as she reached up to cup his face in her hand. "You're the man I've always loved, a man who would never hurt anyone."

Blake pulled away and pushed past her to pace into the room. His heart felt like it was going to burst out of his chest. God, he wanted to believe her, but he couldn't, not after what had brought them back together in the first place.

"That's what you're worried about, isn't it? That you'd hurt me somehow?" she asked. "Well, that's ridiculous. You're not that type of person, you're not Scott. I should—"

"I kidnapped you, Erin. Twice," he said, his shame as thick as it had been two months ago. "Then I tied you down and was going to permanently mark your body, and I only stopped when you started crying so hard I couldn't—"

"So what?" Erin interrupted with a defiant lift of her chin. "You didn't go through with what you'd planned. You didn't hurt me."

"But I could have. And…I might in the future." He sighed. "I've never been in a long-term relationship, period, let alone a Dom-sub long-term relationship. I could be a Scott in the making. I can't promise you I'm not."

"You know why I left Carson City the night after your birthday?" she asked, the abrupt change of subject enough to stun him into silence. "Let me tell you."

Erin wandered toward the kitchen, climbing up on one of the bar stools tucked under the island that separated the living space from the dining space. "Phil had been cornering me for months, on nights when you and Naomi worked late."

"What?" Blake's stomach turned, and he knew he didn't want to hear what Erin was going to say next.

"Sometimes he'd just pin my arms and shove his tongue in my mouth, but sometimes he'd get handsy." Her eyes drifted to the ceiling. "He'd get fingers up my shirt or down my pants. Never for very long, and it never went further than that, but I knew it was only a matter of time. Especially after you moved out. Phil was afraid of you. But once you were gone I knew things would be different...worse."

"Why didn't you tell me?"

"I was ashamed." She sucked in a big breath, eyes still glued to a place above his head as if she couldn't stand to look at him. "And even if I'd told you, I knew there was nothing you could do. Aside from getting yourself thrown in jail."

"You could have gotten transferred to another home," he said. "You could have—"

"There was no guarantee another home would have been any better." Erin laughed bitterly. "You know what it's like, Blake. I had to get out. I couldn't take another two years of Phil or anyone else."

Blake nodded, wanting to take her in his arms, but refusing to let himself touch her. If he started, he might never stop. "I'm sorry. I hope you know now that I wouldn't have thought any less of you. It wasn't your fault. You could have come to me. We would have figured something out without you running off on your own."

"I know that now. And if I could go back..." She met his eyes again with a tight smile. "But I can't and that's not the point to the story."

"What is the point? That the foster care system is seriously flawed?"

"Well, that." She laughed. "And that I always knew Phil was a piece of shit. I had suspicions about Scott, too. I even tried to call off the wedding at one point before he talked me out of it. I didn't know how bad things would get, but I knew we weren't meant to be." She paused, watching him with soft eyes. "But it's different with you. You may not know it, but I do. You're a good man, Blake, and we belong together. Always have, always will."

"Erin, I love you. You know I do, but—"

"I love you, too." She jumped off her chair

and crossed the room, taking his hands in hers. "So there's only one more question that needs to be answered. Well, maybe two questions."

"And what are those?" he asked, feeling his will to fight slipping away. He wanted to believe Erin was right and that he could be the man she needed.

Maybe, with her help, he could be.

"Do you like kids? Abby in particular?" she asked. "Be honest."

"She's the most beautiful thing I've ever seen. I was afraid to hold her too long. I knew if I did, I wouldn't ever want to let her go." Blake paused, still afraid to let hope in. "But if you and I…and Abby… Things would have to change. We'd have to keep the play in the bedroom."

"We would, but that's not such a big deal." Erin smiled, tears filling her eyes. "God, it's so good to hear you say that. About Abby. I'm so glad."

Blake squeezed her hands. "What's the

second question?"

"It's not so much a question as a statement." She sniffed. "Our ticket was one-way. I brought all of our clothes and dropped the few things I had in boxes at the UPS store on the way to the airport. Damned Naughty said I could shoot the layout I'm doing for them as easily in Miami as L.A., and I sort of told my landlord I wouldn't be coming back."

"Sort of?" Blake asked, heart beating faster as he realized the full impact of her words.

"Not sort of, I flat out told him we were out of there. For good." She laughed nervously, her fingers twining in front of her. "And I've got full physical and legal custody of Abby so there's nothing from the past to weigh me down. I want the future. With you. Think you might have room for a couple of girls around the house?"

"A couple?" His eyebrows lifted. "Is Abby—"

"She's in your room," Erin said, gesturing toward the closed door. "There were more pillows in there and I wanted to make sure she didn't roll off the bed if she started moving around in the night. She's a wild sleeper."

"Just like her mother." Blake smiled, barely able to believe this was really happening.

A part of him still felt like he should be fighting the happiness and relief that coursed through his system at the thought of him and Erin and Abby becoming a family, but the rest of him was doing a good job of shutting that insanity down.

Erin was right. They belonged together, for better or worse.

But he was going to do his damnedest to make sure it was all better.

"Yep," Erin said, her smile lighting up her face. "So, you want to get comfortable in the guest room? We could snuggle up in that full bed and see how many times I kick you in my sleep."

"I have a better idea," Blake said, pulling her close, letting his hands travel down to cup her ass.

"Oh?" Erin asked, eyes sparkling. "And what might that be?"

"It seems a shame to waste this outfit you've put on."

"You like it?" she asked as she wrapped her arms around his neck. "I figured you might need a visual aid to remind you how much we belong together. As well as a good talking to."

"An excellent idea. I'm only sorry I didn't have a chance to get prettied up for you."

"That's okay, I kind of dig the beard. Though I've always wondered…" She stood on tiptoe, closing the distance between their lips.

Their first kiss in two months was enough to make Blake's heart threaten to stop beating. The feel of her tongue sneaking into his mouth, the sweet taste of her, the way she dug her fingernails into his neck as their kiss grew more intense—all of it was even more amazing than he remembered.

"Yep, it tickles." She laughed and kissed

him again.

God, there was nothing in the world like kissing this woman. Kissing Erin was like coming home and being transported to another world all at the same time. She was all he'd ever dreamed of and so much more. He was one lucky bastard, and so grateful he hadn't lost her.

"Thank you," he whispered against her lips.

"You're welcome." She sighed as she hugged him more tightly. "I hear sometimes even wise men need a little reality check."

"And you should feel free to give me one anytime."

"I will. But you should feel free to give me things, too." Erin wiggled her bottom under his hands, bringing to mind their last encounter at the club in L.A.

His cock grew even thicker at the thought of private spanking sessions, when there would be no reason not to end the encounter by driving inside Erin's welcoming heat.

Damn, they were going to have fun

together. There were so many things he wanted to do to her, with her, so many boundaries to test and explore.

But tonight, he wanted to keep things simple. "No paddles tonight."

"No?" she asked, looking a little disappointed.

"No, and no nipple clamps or whips or restraints." He kissed her again, softly, thoroughly. "Tonight is about just you and me."

"The real you and me?" she asked, the heat in her eyes making her real question clear.

"Of course." He released her with a smile. "So go get your ass in that bed and spread your legs. Play with my tits and my pussy, but don't touch my clit or come before I get there. Just get my cunt wet. You understand?"

"Yes, sir." She leapt into his arms, hugging him so tight his laugh came out as a grunt, then turned and fled into the guest room.

Blake watched her go with an ache in his chest so strong he could barely breathe.

That was his girl. His love, the only woman who would ever know him, who could ever make him feel like he was the kind of man he wanted to be. And he was going to do whatever it took to show her how much she meant to him—tonight and every night for the rest of their lives.

He stopped and took a deep breath before following her, his eyes drawn down to the angel on his arm. For a moment, he would have sworn the ink looked brighter, richer than it had in years, as if the tat itself were grateful to be reunited with the woman who matched him as perfectly as their identical tattoos.

CHAPTER SEVENTEEN

Erin

As she ran and jumped onto the guest bed, Erin felt like laughing and crying at the same time.

She'd done it; she'd really done it! And it hadn't been nearly as hard as she'd worried it would be.

Her stomach had been tied in knots for the entire plane ride. Not even Abby's constant squirming on her lap could distract her from her fear that Blake's stubbornness would prove too much for her to conquer. Once he had his mind made up, he was usually impossible to sway.

But then, neither of them had ever been in love like this. What they'd felt for each other when they were kids had been wonderful and real, but nothing compared to the connection they had now. This was what people dreamed about, wrote stories and made movies about. This was the real thing, a love she hadn't dared dream she'd find.

The thought was enough to bring fresh tears to her eyes.

"Disobeying my first order. This doesn't bode well for our future," Blake said, the laughter in his voice making her smile.

"You're the one who said I was a pushy bottom." Erin rolled over onto her back, her breath catching as she saw him standing in the door, wearing nothing but his jeans. How many times had she fantasized about that bare chest? About running her fingers over the contours of his muscles, letting her tongue trace each dip and curve?

"I was wrong, you're not pushy, just hard to handle." He stalked slowly toward the bed, making her pulse pound.

"I'll probably need a lot of discipline and punishment before I'm anywhere near where I should be." Erin spread her legs, slowly, deliberately, and let her fingers trail up her thigh. She was already wet and aching, just seeing Blake was enough to make her body come to life. "Training me is not going to be an easy job."

Blake watched her hand with undisguised fascination as she slid her fingers inside her thong, dipping into the well of heat between her legs. "Easy is overrated." His breath rushed out through his parted lips. "I can't believe you're here."

"I'm here and I'm never going to leave," Erin said, the back of her throat getting tight again. "Now are you going to fuck me or not?

If not, I'm probably going to start crying again and I've really had about all the—"

"Take off your panties. Leave the stockings and shoes on."

Erin obeyed, hands shaking as she quickly shed the scrap of silk and then lay back on the bed, her nipples so hard they poked through the stiff satin of her corset. A wave of dizzying desire swept over her from head to toe, making her head spin. God, she needed this, needed Blake to take control of her, to make her feel so safe and free and completely consumed by him.

Him. Her love. Her perfect match.

Every name she called him made her giddier.

"Spread your legs. Wider," Blake ordered, working at his belt with swift, sure movements. "Show me my pussy."

Electricity shot through her entire body as she parted her thighs. She could feel her lips plump under his eyes, swelling until she felt bruised with the force of her wanting. She sure as hell hoped Blake wasn't planning some long, drawn-out seduction, because she didn't think her mind would survive it. She needed him.

Now.

They could do the long, drawn-out thing later, when she didn't feel so desperate for the connection she'd been denied for the past two months.

"You are so beautiful," he said, his voice catching as he shoved jeans and boxer briefs to the floor, freeing his cock. The poor man was so swollen the veins stood up along his length, and his plump head dripped a single sticky tear.

Erin licked her lips—she wanted to taste that salty drop, to lick it away and suck his beautiful cock deep between her lips. "You, too. You don't know how many times I've imagined this."

"I can guess." He knelt at the edge of the bed, bringing his warm hands to the inside of her thighs and spreading her wider. "Maybe a few hundred less than I have. I swear to God, I could taste you in my sleep."

"Please, Blake." She squirmed beneath him, feeling she would shatter if he didn't shove that beautiful hardness between her legs in the next ten seconds. "I need you inside of me."

"Are you topping from the bottom again?" he asked, his voice soft as he dipped one thumb into her cunt, groaning as he slowly drove in and out of her slick heat.

"No, I just—"

"Because if you are, I don't care. Nothing could keep me from fucking this pussy." He slid his hands from her body and positioned his cock at her entrance in one smooth movement. "Right now."

She called his name as his hips surged forward, shoving his engorged length inside her. There was a hint of resistance at first. No matter how aroused she was, he was a tight fit, his cock even thicker, harder, hotter than it usually was. He felt so large that a hint of delicious pain accompanied her pleasure as he filled her, driving fast and deep, not stopping until he lay buried to the hilt.

"God, Erin." His breath came in swift, shallow puffs against her lips as she wrapped her arms and legs around him, pulling him closer. "I'm not going to last five minutes. You feel so fucking good."

"Five minutes should be more than enough." She rolled her hips in a slow circle, grinding her clit into his pelvic bone with a shuddering sigh. "You feel pretty good yourself."

"I aim to please," he said as his hands gripped the top of her corset and tugged, pulling at the fabric until her breasts were free. "I missed these tits."

"And I missed you calling them tits. I actually came to like the—" She broke off with a soft cry.

Oh, God, his tongue. She couldn't remember anything feeling as good as his tongue flicking across her nipples. Her hips circled faster as shocks of awareness surged between her legs.

"Nothing tastes like your skin, nothing in the world." Blake mumbled the words against her breast before he sucked one nipple into his mouth, tugging at the aroused flesh until she cried out. "So fucking sweet."

"Please, Blake, please," Erin panted, tugging at his hair.

It was too much, more stimulation than her overly sensitized body could take, especially since he refused to move inside her. He still lay buried in her pulsing sheath, pinning her to the mattress with his weight, limiting her movement to those little rolls of her hips that just weren't enough.

She needed him to fuck her, to slam his cock in and out of her pussy until it hurt, until that brutal penetration sent her spiraling into the bliss only Blake could give her.

"Please!" She pulled at him with all her strength, but he simply removed her hands, pressing her wrists into the pillow above her head as he transferred his maddening attentions to her other nipple.

"Don't say another word until I'm finished with my tits." Blake accentuated his words by dragging his teeth across her aching tip, making her scream.

Erin bit her lip and moaned as he moved from one breast to another, slowly driving her insane, making her pussy gush liquid heat as it clutched at his thickness.

She was so close to the edge but unable to tumble over. She couldn't come, not without his approval, not even if she'd wanted to.

Which she didn't. More than release, more than relief, she wanted to please Blake. No matter how hard to handle she might be, that part of her was a submissive through and through.

Blake's submissive. Her body belonged to him, for now, for always.

The thought made her even hotter, wilder, until her legs churned on either side of Blake's.

"My pussy is so wet. I love feeling my

pussy so wet," he said, before sucking one nipple deep into his mouth and letting his teeth bite down on the soft flesh of her breast. The pressure grew greater and greater, until the trapped flesh began to sting.

God, he was going to mark her. There would be an imprint of his teeth on her breast by the time he pulled away. Just imagining her pale flesh bearing the sign of his possession threatened to undo her. She wanted to scream, to beg, to cry out his name, but she bit her lip, struggling to obey his request for silence as he set about marking her other breast.

Her head tossed back and forth on the pillow and she fought Blake's hold on her wrists until her muscles ached, but there was no relief to be found. He was in complete control and would continue his erotic torture until he was good and ready to stop. The knowledge both thrilled and frightened her, forcing a desperate sob from her throat.

Finally, when she was certain her sanity

couldn't hold a second longer, Blake called her name, the abandon in the sound letting her know he'd reached the same razor-sharp edge. With a sound more animal than human, he drew back until only the tip of his cock was inside her and then rammed back in, setting a swift, brutal pace that was exactly what her body had been craving.

Erin cried out as he released his hold on her wrists, wild to feel her nails digging into the muscles of his back. She wanted to mark him the same way he'd marked her, to leave behind traces of their passion that would follow him for days, so that every time he felt that slight sting or saw that trail of red, he would think of her, of the way they were together, here where they belonged.

They were meant to be connected like this, fused so tightly it was impossible to tell where his body ended and hers began. They were a part of each other, a matched pair that would never be separated again. Just like their tattoos, the things that had brought them back together in the first place.

It no longer seemed strange that she'd been so resistant to having her angel modified. The night they'd acquired their matching ink was the night they'd promised each other the future. She didn't want to lose the symbol of that beautiful night, not now, not ever.

"God, I love you, Erin," he panted. "I love you so much."

"Me, too, so much. So much." She gasped the words into his mouth as he took her lips in a brutal kiss, mating his tongue with hers as his rhythm grew even faster, frantic, until she knew he was only seconds away from losing control. An answering wildness rose within her, tightening things low in her body, making every muscle tremble with the prelude to her own release.

She ripped her mouth from his, the room spinning as she fought to hold back the dark wave threatening to pull her under. "Please!"

"Erin, God, Erin." Faster and faster, until the sound of skin making contact with skin filled the room, until her every nerve cried out with the need to come, to find her pleasure around the thickness working between her thighs.

"I'm going to come. I can't help it, I'm—"

"Come, Erin. God, come for me." He groaned and his entire body shuddered as his cock began to pulse within her.

Erin joined him a second later, her body bowing off the bed with the force of her release. Her womb contracted again and again, the orgasm so fierce it made her dizzy. Her nails dug into Blake's back and her heels into the mattress as pure bliss rocketed through her body, making her sob and tears of happiness leak from behind her closed lids.

When she finally drifted back to earth, she was shocked to find she was laughing.

And not just kind of laughing, but giggling so hard the tightening of her muscles had forced Blake's softening length from her body and her sides were starting to hurt.

Blake's rumble of laughter underscored her

own as he rolled to lie beside her. "What kind of woman gets the giggles after sex like that?"

"I don't know." She laughed even harder, rolling on her side and clutching at her stomach. "God, that was great."

"It was," he said, gazing down at her with an amused expression.

"I love you so much," she gasped, the giggle fit showing no signs of stopping.

"Good thing I'm a confident man or this might be doing something to my self-esteem."

That was all it took to make her lose it. She laughed until her head hurt and her body ached, until it was hard to breathe and she contracted a serious case of the hiccups. She honestly didn't know when she would have stopped if Abby hadn't cried out from the other room.

"Oh, no, the baby's awake," she said, pressing her hands into her sore jaw muscles as she finally regained control.

"I'm guessing it was the crazy woman laughing in the other room who woke her up, what do you think?" Blake was already out of bed, pulling pajama pants from a drawer and throwing her a tee shirt.

"Or it could have been the screaming orgasm."

"We're going to have to invest in some soundproof walls before this kid gets any older." He smiled as he spoke, his excitement for the future—their future—clear on his face. "Do you think she'd let me pick her up and bring her in here with us?"

"I don't think she'd mind at all." Erin smiled, fighting back the tears in her eyes. No more crazy laughing or crying. At least not tonight anyway. "I'll turn down the bed."

She shrugged on the oversize tee shirt and found her underpants on the floor. She'd dressed, used the restroom, and put order to the bed by the time Blake came back into the room, holding a blinking Abby. She looked confused, but not unhappy to be in Blake's arms.

"She was wet, so I changed her with one of

the diapers by the bed. I think I got it on right, but you might want to check," he said, the uncertainty on his face making her want to hug him.

Erin reached out and took Abby before climbing into the bed. "I'm sure it's fine."

"Maybe, but I'm going to need practice. It took me at least three minutes. Good thing she was patient with me." Blake took his place on the other side of the bed, smiling down at Abby as Erin placed her on the sheets between them.

The baby immediately started to nuzzle into the covers, making happy cooing noises.

"She's always loved sleeping with someone," Erin said. "I know I should make her sleep by herself, but I can't bring myself to put her back in her crib when she wakes up in the night."

"What if I roll over and crush her?" Blake asked, inching as close to the opposite edge of the bed as possible.

"You won't," Erin said, leaning over to

press a soft kiss to his lips. "And this will just be for tonight. We'll buy her a crib tomorrow."

"A crib sounds good." Blake smiled against her lips. "I mean, I wouldn't mind the family sleeping thing. But it might make it hard to do certain things."

"Right. And we like those things. Games are fun."

He laughed. "I wasn't thinking about games, but yeah, I like those, too."

"What were you thinking about?" She sighed into her pillow, certain she couldn't feel happier than she did right now, freshly bedded by the man she loved and snuggled in with her two favorite people in the world.

"I was thinking about maybe…making a brother or sister someday. I mean, not too soon, but—"

"As soon as you're ready," Erin said, breaking her vow not to get teary again. "I can't think of anything more exciting."

"Not even investing in a spanking bench of

our very own?" Blake smiled, but even in the dim light she could see the telltale shine in his eyes.

"Not even a spanking bench of my very own. Though I want one of those, too." She smiled. "I can balance babies and spankings. Don't you think?"

"I think you can do anything you set your mind to." Blake reached out to touch her face, careful not to disturb Abby, who was already asleep again. "I love you, Erin."

"I love you, too."

He was out a few minutes later, his deep, steady breathing lulling her into a state of profound relaxation.

Still, she fought sleep as long she was able, wanting to savor these moments, the beginning of her life with the man who had forever claimed her heart.

** The End **

Sign up for Lili's newsletter to receive a
FREE sneak peak of Lili's next erotic trilogy,
coming summer of 2015:

http://eepurl.com/bdEzTb

LILI VALENTE

Acknowledgements

I really do have so many people to thank, so please forgive my gushing in advance.

Big thanks to my husband, my biggest fan and most tireless supporter. You believed I could do this when not many people did. Love you hard man, forever and ever. Let's never go our separate ways.

Thank you to my critique partners (the most patient women in the world) for reading numerous drafts and never getting tired of Erin and Blake (or at least not letting me know they were tired of them).

Thank you to my editor, proofers, and sweet and lovely cover designer—this wouldn't have been possible without you!

Big huge thanks to all the readers out there. You are rock stars. The way you go above and beyond to support the authors you enjoy is truly amazing and so appreciated. Much, much love and endless thanks for embracing a newbie and making me one of your own.

Mad thanks to Kara H. for keeping me organized and on task. Without your help, professionalism, and all around awesome the launch for the Under His Command series wouldn't have gone one fifth as smoothly. You are the best!

Thanks to all the early reviewers who took a chance on Controlling Her Pleasure. I appreciate your time and effort to post ratings and reviews so much.

Finally a few special shout outs:

To my street team: You are the sweetest, naughtiest, book-loving-est people ever and I feel so lucky to have you in my life.

To Lauren Blakely who is a genius and a talent and just as importantly, a woman with a kind and generous heart. Thanks for being a friend and inspiration.

To Monica Murphy. Who would have thought we'd be here when we met in 2005? Can't wait to hang out with you again soon and soak up more of that signature MM sweetness and sass.

To Sawyer Bennett, a talented and generous new friend who constantly inspires me to be a better, more chill person. You make it look easy, doll.

To Violet Duke for the amazing cover design, friendship, and support—even though I write naughty books and yours are so sweet and wonderful they make me laugh and cry in equal measure. You are a blessing to all who know you and that's the truth.

To Robin, friend and editorial guru, you make me laugh and keep my commas under control. Without you I would wander in the darkness of WTF punctuation-ville.

To my mother, who told to me to write whatever I wanted to write and pay no attention to the naysayers. What a lucky chick I am to have a mama like you.

To my father, who didn't live to meet my husband, babies, or book babies, but who raised me to believe I could do whatever I set my mind to, as long as I was willing to work hard and never give up. Thank you, Dad. You are missed more than you know.

And on a much lighter note, thank you to all the makers of chocolate in all its wondrous forms. You lift me up on days when the sun doesn't shine.

Tell Lili your favorite part!

Lili loves feedback from her readers. If you could take a moment to leave a review letting her know your favorite part of the story—nothing fancy required, even a sentence or two would be wonderful—she would be deeply grateful. Reviews are so important and help other readers discover new authors and series to enjoy.

LILI VALENTE

About the Author

Lili Valente started writing naughty books in her early twenties as a way to unwind after a long day in the day job trenches. She soon learned there was nothing more fun than torturing fictional characters who have dynamite chemistry in the bedroom.

After a prolonged detour through other areas of writing and publishing—including a short stint as a news reporter for a small town paper—she's back to penning red hot stories and loving every minute of it.

She lives on an island in the middle of nowhere, where she eats entirely too much fish and drinks more than her fair share of dark, island rum.

Lili has slept under the stars in Greece,

eaten dinner at midnight with French men who couldn't be trusted to keep their mouths on their food, and walked alone through Munich's red light district after dark and lived to tell the tale.

These days you can find her writing in a tent beside the sea, drinking coconut water and thinking delightfully dirty thoughts.

Lili loves to hear from her readers.!

You can reach her via email at lili.valente.romance@gmail.com

Or like her page on Facebook https://www.facebook.com/AuthorLiliVal ente?ref=hl

You can also visit her website: www.lilivalente.com

Or sign up for her newsletter here:

http://bit.ly/1zXpwL6

CPSIA information can be obtained at www.ICGtesting.com
Printed in the USA
BVOW06s1319250515

401651BV00018B/543/P